Cul De Sac

Cul De Sac

Scott Wrobel

Sententia Books
Brooklyn, NY 2012

Cul De Sac by Scott Wrobel

Sententia Books
www.SententiaBooks.com
84 Dean Street
Brooklyn, NY 11201

ISBN: 978-0-9838790-1-5

These stories are a work of fiction. Names, characters, places and incidents are the products of the author's imagination or are used fictitiously, and any resemblance to any persons, living or dead, events or locales, is entirely coincidental. An excerpt from the song "After the Lovin'" by Engelbert Humperdinck appears in "After the Lovin'."

Sententia Books also publishes *Sententia, The Journal*.

Some of these stories have appeared, sometimes in different form, in the following publications: *Burnt Aluminum, Great River Review, Identity Theory, Night Train, Pindeldyboz (web), The Rake,* and *Sententia*.

For my father, Chuck Wrobel (1932-2008). He introduced me to Benny Hill. I took it from there.

"Well cared-for homes
tell a positive story about a neighborhood."
Community Welcome Guide

Cul De Map

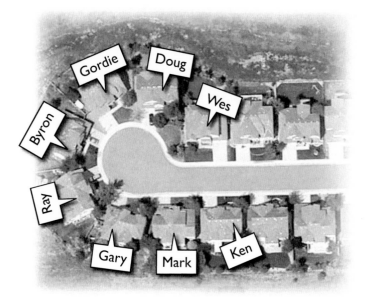

Cul-de-sac, n.   \'kul-di-sak

1. a blind diverticulum or pouch
2. a street or passage closed at one end
3. a route or course leading nowhere

French, literally, the bottom of the bag (1738)

.

Contents

Part One
Regular Guys

Motor Repair   1

After the Lovin'   17

Model Man   37

Animals in Distress   57

Regular Guy   83

Part Two
The Ballad of Gary Wiegard

Where the Kids Go   103

Peckers   123

Swimming   139

Engravings   185

The World at War   205

Storage (2003)   221

Acknowledgements   235

Part One

Regular Guys

Motor Repair

Ken and his family get invited to this lake place owned by a guy named Bob D. who Ken's been going to A.A. meetings with. As the sun falls behind the trees across the lake, Ken and his wife Tanya and Bob D. and his wife sit in lawn chairs. The husbands drink non-alcoholic Sharp's beers and the wives drink Miller Lites, and they're looking at the glassy, calm lake when Bob says, "Can you hear that?"

"I don't hear anything," Tanya says.

But then a soft hum turns to a purr and then a growl, and from behind a peninsula appears a wooden speedboat so varnished it reflects the sun like a camera flash, and the strong sound of its motor stuns Ken.

"Jesus," he whispers.

"It's lovely," Bob says. "Have you ever heard anything so beautiful?"

Ken and Bob D. are sober-buddies. They never drank together. That's why Bob D. can say "lovely" and "beautiful" to Ken and not get punched, the same with the biker guys at the meetings who hug Ken all the time.

"Sounds like noise to me," says Tanya, smirking. "Motors drive me nuts." She takes a hit off her beer. Ken's heart pounds in his ears and he wraps his fist tight around his Sharp's bottle like it's the most important thing in the world, and then his son Robby, still in his swimsuit at sunset, runs onto the dock and drops a load of white landscaping rocks into the water. Then he runs back up the hill for more.

"What are you doing?" Tanya yells.

"I'm Conveyor-Belt-Man-Guy," Robby yells back while running at a full sprint.

Tanya leans over to Ken and whispers loud enough so everyone can hear:

"Maybe you should go control your son."

The next morning, Ken stands at the kitchen sink drinking coffee and watching Gary across the street pressure-wash his garage floor with a Coleman Power Mate. Ken is thinking about buying one himself. Gary is down on his hands and knees, holding the nozzle at an angle so a beam of concentrated spray penetrates the cement. The water strikes so hard it evaporates in the air like steam.

Ken's been up all night, first because he drank too much coffee on the drive home from Bob D.'s, and then Robby had nightmares about skeleton pirates, and then the neighborhood's sick kid got sick again. The neighbors, Mark and Laura, have a one-year-old named Mitchell who's getting a kidney transplant in a month. Last night at midnight, the ambulance came because Mitchell turned blue again. Sometimes he stops breathing. The flashing lights kept Ken up. Still no word on what happened. No one is back at the house and Mark left for work again early. He sped off in his Comcast Communications van. He's a wireless network technician. He replaces burnt-out routers.

Last week, Mark came over to Ken's house because Robby's ceiling fan died. Robby had been turning the switch on and off like a strobe light until he got bored and started playing basketball with stuffed toys and a laundry basket, so Ken took the light off, checked the ceiling and switch connections, blew a circuit and said, "I have no goddamn idea," as Tanya talked on the phone with Mark's wife Laura.

"I'll have Mark come over," Tanya said. "Laura said he's got some kind of electrical license."

Ken wanted to yell, "Mark's got more important problems," but instead he said, "I can fix it myself."

Twenty minutes later, Mark brought over his digital multi-meter, which looked like a walkie-talkie with two wires sticking from the top, to measure the line voltage.

"You want a beer?" Ken asked him. Tanya still kept beer in the refrigerator because she wanted to be able to have a beer "every now and then" even though Ken didn't want any around because it made him perspire.

"I can't drink," Mark said. "I'm getting my kidney clean."

"I thought alcohol ruined the liver."

"The liver and kidney work together. I'm not a big reader or anything, but I just read some articles about kidney transplants." Mark looked down and sighed so loud that Ken thought he was going to start crying, so Ken thought about making a joke about being able to assemble a motorcycle blindfolded the way Fonzie could in *Happy Days* but not being able to get a light to work in his kid's room, but he couldn't think of a way to make it funny.

After Mark inspected the light switch, he pulled away the multi-meter, wrapped the cords around it and shrugged, signaling the kids to come back in and play. Robby had some kind of car and truck building-block set-up. Then Laura carried Baby Mitchell up the stairs, set him on the carpet and handed Mark a black backpack.

"You got current," Mark said. "That much we know."

"Must be the switch," Ken said. A clear thin tube poked from between the buttons on Mitchell's blue one-piece footie jammies, and Ken guessed the backpack on Mark's shoulders wasn't full of baby bottles and diapers but a portable IV machine. A four-foot tube snaked into the kid's belly and a smaller tube snaked out. They looked like fish tank hoses, the kind used to transport oxygen bubbles into aquariums. Ken had a tube into his own gut, too, but thinner, from his glossy new insulin pump.

Mitchell rolled on the floor, grabbing at Lego pieces, and then lay down with the tubes wrapped around his back. Ken wanted to ask Mark how it felt to have to give up an organ for your kid, but instead he asked him if the IV machine took lithium batteries like his insulin pump. He wanted to give Mark a brotherly hug like the guys at the meetings, but instead he tried to make a joke: "Say,

Mark, can a guy get a wireless insulin pump? I hate this tube taped into my gut. It itches all the time."

Mark looked down.

"Wireless insulin access," Ken repeated, trying to make the joke happen, but Mark just looked down at the kids, and after a clumsy silence, Ken said, "Well, I guess it's back to the old drawing board on this light deal."

Ken's in the middle of this outpatient treatment program with a bunch of other court-ordered drunks because six weeks ago he got off his shift at the hospital where he works as a lead maintenance technician, had too many beers at an Applebee's bar, drove his Harley Heritage Softail into a row of mailboxes, and ended up concussed on some guy's driveway. Then he went to jail for a night, lost his license, entered an outpatient treatment program, and during the admission physical he got diagnosed with diabetes. It's like he went into one of those magician's disappearing boxes but the trick backfired and he came out with feet growing from his skull. A wave of the wand and he's a diabetic alcoholic. He's also a husband and a father. He's also 40 years old and his blood sugar is too high.

"Your blood sugar is over four hundred," the doctor said.

"Okay," said Ken. "Does a guy want a higher number like in basketball or a lower number like in golf?"

"I'm not understanding the question."

That night after the doctor, while in the living room watching TV, Ken told Tanya he had a drinking problem and diabetes. She said, "You're being dramatic. You just need to stop after two beers like I do."

She stood and went to bed.

"Diabetes," Ken said. "I can't process sugar." But she was already down the hallway.

Ken lay on the couch and watched a special on late-night TV about Brazilian kids with deformed mouths. Then he lay down next to his sleeping son. Robby's nerves and muscles flinched, elbows and knees twitching like an epileptic. Ken went back to the couch.

The next day, Ken was back at the clinic again, but this time for a behavioral consult for Robby. When the nurse asked Robby to sit on the exam table, he jumped up on the edge and kicked his heels back into the metal drawers like he was trying to kill them. Ken and Tanya talked with the doctor, whose name was Mary Brooks, while Robby squirmed over the gray exam table, and in his frenzied movement, twisted up the sheet of sanitary paper that covered the gray rubbery fabric, caught a tennis shoe tip underneath it, and ended up with paper folded over him like a badly wrapped present.

"He gets bored easy," Ken said, and Mary Brooks stared at him hard and said, "He's not moving around like that because he's bored. He's moving around because his brain can't control his body." She talked like Robby couldn't hear her, like he couldn't process the conversation because his brain skittered from one thought to the next like he had defective sparkplugs in his head. "I don't want to get too far ahead here, folks, but there's no reason to be afraid of medication. Everyone has an opinion about it, even if they don't have kids with ADHD. Let me simplify it for you. The thing with ADHD kids is that their motor is running all the time. Would you say Robby's motor is running all the time?"

When she mentioned the motor, Ken thought of how his Harley Davidson sounded just before he plowed into the mailboxes: loud. And how it sounded when the bike was flipping across the lawn: a loose, diarrheic fart. Then he thought about the power washer his neighbor Gary just bought, how strong it sounded. And he imagined his eight-year-old son as a soccer hooligan with a shaved skull that he used as a weapon to head-butt guys in moldy bars.

Robby's head was now at the foot of the exam table. He reached his arms out from under the wrapping paper and clutched the stirrups that women parked their heels in for vaginal exams. He made "vroom" noises and moved the metal bars in and out like he was running a backhoe.

On the drive home, Tanya's forehead crinkled so deeply that Ken thought of saying "Botox". She turned to him and said, "I want this kid on drugs. Now."

Ken looked into the back seat and Robby seemed serene, hands on his lap, head forward, looking upward out the window as though taking in the sight of a soaring hawk or a spreading jet contrail.

"Did you see him crawling around in there? Did you not notice that? I am so tired."

"Okay."

"He's going on drugs. I'm done."

Robby stared out the window, contemplating the sublime beauty of the sky.

One day after the morning counseling session, Tanya picked Ken up to have lunch in the parking lot of the Super America. As day manager at a Great Clips, Tanya called her own shots about taking breaks. Her favorite food was the egg-salad sandwich from Super America. It was wrapped in six layers of Saran Wrap. When she peeled it open and exposed the sandwich to oxygen, it smelled the way a chicken farm smelled from a half mile away.

A gay guy with a butt-sway walked into the Super America, probably to pay for gas or buy a packaged salad, and Tanya said, "Why would a guy want to be like that?"

"What do you mean?"

"Who'd want to get made fun of all the time? I feel sorry for those guys."

"Maybe it's not a choice."

"Everything's a choice," she said. "Everyone makes their own bed."

Ken got what she meant, that people had free will. That his being a booze addict was a choice. All he had to do was drink fewer beers.

He'd tried to convince Tanya he didn't have a choice by taking her to an evening program at the hospital where he went to treatment. They'd sat in a small auditorium that smelled like unguent. On the video screen played a movie that explained alcoholism as a disease, with diagrams of the human brain and arrows pointing to different colored regions, and if a certain region was a certain color, say, red, it was a part of the brain that sent a signal to the rest of the brain that more alcohol was needed, and then what happened was a chain reaction of liquor-hunger throughout the nervous system.

Tanya had squinted like she needed glasses.

The narrator said, "Though alcoholism is a disease that the alcoholic has no control over, managing the disease is still possible through a lifetime of daily maintenance."

Tanya had leaned over and whispered, "I don't buy it. It's a choice." She got up and left and Ken followed. She'd lit a cigarette when the electronic doors slid open and Ken said roughly, "If you don't stay until the end of this, we're done."

"Lose the tough guy shit. You lost your leverage when you got the DWI."

"Okay."

So now Ken's in the passenger seat in the parking lot of Super America with his wife eating her egg salad and telling him everything was a choice, and he wanted to yell, but he had a knot in his throat like a pill jammed in his esophagus, so instead he mumbled, "I love you."

"Me too," said Tanya, starting up the motor.

According to this book Ken has to read for his program, he and his wife are supposed to say they love each other at least three times a day, like flossing. They'll go full guns for two weeks and then get lazy about it, like life after a motivational seminar.

Ken hasn't slept all night since getting back from Bob D.'s. He tries to measure his feelings the way he measures the miles per gallon on his truck, but the math isn't working, so instead he drinks more coffee and listens to the hum of the vacuum in his head and Gary's air compressor. Last night, the flickering lights of another emergency run for Baby Mitchell made his brain chemicals expand. Here's what's funny: he's so full of caffeine he can hear the blood moving through his ears. Not his pulse—he can always hear that—but the actual sound of the liquid carving through his capillaries like muddy water through sandstone. He can hear everything. As he stands at the kitchen window and watches Gary pressure wash his garage floor, he can hear the breathing of the air hose, even through the growl of the motor that drives the air compressor. It sounds like the hiss of the nebulizer they use for Robby because he has lungs like paper maché.

Once they had to go to the emergency room because Robby almost stopped breathing. He was sprinting around the perimeter of the house, over and over, until he collapsed and wheezed, and he wouldn't stop wheezing. At the hospital, Ken and Tanya crammed into a space surrounded by a curtain and a cement wall with shelves of medical supplies: gauze, jars of jellies and compresses, rubber gloves. Robby sat on the edge of an exam table as a young doctor who smelled like toothpaste slid a stethoscope over his back and glanced up into the fluorescent beam, puzzling a diagnosis.

"He's not breathing too good," the doctor said. He rested his left hand on Robby's shoulder and circled the scope around his back with his right. "You'll want to avoid temperature extremes in cases like this."

"Cases like this?" Tanya said. "What is *this*?"

"Tight lungs." The doctor squinted.

"What does that mean?"

"It's tough to say right now." The doctor lifted the stethoscope. "We need a culture, and for that we need him to cough up some fluid, but his fluid is pretty solid. We'll get him on antibiotics. If it's a virus we might have to rethink options. Keep an eye on him for the next couple of days and bring him in if he doesn't improve, but I don't see that happening."

"See *what* happening?" Tanya asked.

"Needing to bring him back in." The doctor yawned and waved it away. "Go ahead and put his shirt on. The nurse will be back with a prescription, and we'll send a nebulizer home with you." He mussed Robby's hair and his head swayed across his weak neck. The doctor parted the curtain and disappeared.

Tanya squeezed Ken's bicep. "Why didn't you stop him? He didn't say anything."

"I'm tired."

Truth is, Ken likes it when Robby gets sick because he sleeps or sprawls on the couch watching TV, and then so can Ken. When he isn't sick, he's running in place, jumping on chairs, sprinting through rooms snaring objects and shifting them to other rooms, banging sticks against the driveway or garage door, collecting rocks—

not fancy or particular rocks, just any, including chunks of concrete and sticky bits of blacktop—and piling them in his closet. And at night, he wails unless they read him stories, maintain constant noise and light: humidifier fan, ceiling fan, Sounds of Nature CDs, three night-lights. Silence and darkness mean death to Robby. His room is a casino. Imagine a kid who sleeps maybe four, at most, five hours a night for the first six years of his life, his parents having to hold his hands and rub his forehead, sing songs and read books in soft voices, and when it's three a.m. and Dad's already hammered and has to be to work in four hours and Robby's screaming that he wants to go outside and play, no shit, he's yelling, "Sleep is boring!" Ken stomps to the kitchen, cuts opens a Benadryl allergy caplet containing 50 milligrams of Dipenhydramine, squeezes the sap into a cup of water and delivers it to the boy, like treason.

Wireless insulin injection, motors, pumps, tubes. Ken wonders what the world sounds like behind all the motor noise. Even at night he needs a fan next to his head or else all he can hear is his caffeinated heart battering like a drum solo. He tries not to think about heavy things, but he can't stop worrying about Robby, who walks on top of monkey bars with his eyes closed, grabs electric fences and laughs. Whenever he sees a retaining wall, he does a backflip off it. The kid is the way he is because of Ken. They're hardwired. Naming him after Robert "Evel" Knievel didn't help. Heroic measures won't keep Ken's boy from steering a wheelchair with his chin and taking leaks through a tube.

Ken burns glucose by chasing down Robby, keeping him off the street, away from construction sites. He tests his blood sugar and makes sure he presses the right numbers on the machine strapped to his belt. That's his main job, to not run out of juice.

Robby, meanwhile, has plenty of juice. His motor's always running. After the doctor visit, Ken and Tanya sent Robby up to his room so they could sit at the kitchen table and fill out surveys. They read the questions about whether Robby was distractible, argued with adults, cried without reason. Did he have trouble sleeping at night? Did he complain about feeling unloved, that nobody liked him? It asked if he abused animals, fought with peers, resisted school, avoided eating, was easily fatigued, restless, agitated. Did he lie, cheat, steal? Did he lose things? Did he have a hard time playing quietly? Did it seem like his "motor" was running all the time?

Tanya answered "Almost Always" to every question, but Ken answered "Almost Always" to only two, the ones about not sleeping and the motor. Upstairs, items plummeted from shelves in Robby's room. They heard his footsteps and fast breathing, the boy's chest huffing like an air compressor, which reminded Ken that two months earlier, in August, Gary let Mark use his air compressor to pressure-wash his vinyl siding. For the whole weekend, Mark blasted out dirt, mold, spider webs and bird shit from the crevices between panels. He never went in the house, probably because Baby Mitchell was in there sleeping, exhausted, his blood unclean from his weak kidney. Laura walked outside and brought Mark juice and water because he needed a clean kidney to give to Mitchell, and Ken walked over to say how clean he thought his house was getting and "what a great goddamn air compressor, Mark."

"It's Gary's," Mark said. "He bought it. I'm borrowing it."

And Ken remembered the night Baby Mitchell had rolled all over Robby's floor, twisting and pinching the tube, and Robby trying to hold him still, Robby actually trying to hold someone else still.

"Articles on kidney transplants catch my eye," Mark said. He kneeled and untangled the cords, lifting Mitchell a bit and pulling the tubes forward under his legs and up over his feet. "I read this one about this felon who gave up his kidney for a kid and the article brought up this guy's past, all the shit he did wrong, instead of just saying hey, here's a guy who's trying to do something good, you know?"

When Mark talked about the felon paying penance, Ken had thought he was sending him a message, and he wanted to tell Mark he was a hero for giving a kidney to his son. Ken wanted to hug him, but instead he said, "Man, Gary has a killer air compressor," and Mark told the story about borrowing the compressor to wash his house: "I thought maybe there was mold in the cracks and that was bothering Mitchell, making him so tired all the time." Mark had clamped his mouth shut and looked down at Mitchell, who sat upright, smiling at Robby.

"You wanna see my Star Wars guys?" said Robby, and

Ken maybe thought it was okay to pack some clothes and his A.A. Big Book into a backpack, hop on a bicycle, and go find a studio apartment close to work with a beerless refrigerator and he could pay a little extra for a garage, where he could fix up his broken motorcycle.

Gary power-washes his garage floor through the morning, working his way toward the driveway, and before noon, Ken is playing catch with Robby in the yard. Every time Robby attempts to catch the ball, he dives dramatically, misses and rolls on the grass, flips back up, retrieves the ball and rifles it hard back at Ken, throwing it over his head and then jumping up and down, pounding his glove while Ken chases it down through pine tree branches and throws it back to him so he can re-create a spectacular miss again. Ken drinks water and checks his blood sugar and eats granola bars when his glucose gets low. This is how Saturday goes.

Ken could listen to Gary's Coleman Powermate pressure washer forever, its hum attractive and strong, like the sound of the engine that spins the planet, like the grumble of a Harley. Mark probably sees the air compressor more as a means to wash his siding, though, to stay outdoors, away from the inside where Mitchell goes from laughing to gagging and then there's an ambulance parked in the driveway and Laura and Mitchell are in the back and it's late at night and Mark knows he has to get up and work in the morning, so he asks his boss if he can just bring his repair truck home, and his boss understands, and so Mark sits in the garage on a lawn chair next to the truck until two a.m. on a Saturday morning waiting for the cell phone to ring and when he gets a call, it's hopefully only some folks losing their wireless connection, and so as Ken watches Gary power-wash his garage floor, he also watches Mark back out of his driveway and head down Eagle Street, his garage door dropping behind him like a stage curtain.

After the Lovin'

There are many reasons for my admiration of Engelbert Humperdinck: first, for forty years and thousands of after-concert parties with ladies offering themselves to him, "The Enge" has remained faithful to his true love, Patricia; second, the spectacular voice and stage presence; and third, the significant moustache he sported in the '80s and which I myself sported in my early twenties while trying to attract a mate. That's when I met my wife Betty, who has the condition of "morbid" or "gross" obesity, and such is the reason why every morning my first ritual is hoisting Betty's bedpan to the bathroom. Then I take a shower and croon optimistic water-backed tunes such as "Quando Quando Quando" and "Up, Up and Away," which readies me for another crappy day.

Betty spends most of her time in bed since she lost circulation in her extremities. Her legs look like the husky slabs of beef that hang from hooks in packing houses, like the ones Rocky punched when he trained. When I get out of the shower, I transport Betty to the kitchen table in a modified wheelchair and help her to shift over onto a reinforced chair, which makes her feel somewhat normal, and then I park the wheelchair in the bedroom until I have to transport her back to the bed.

Betty squints through glucose-clouded eyes at a book called *How Low-Fat Diets Make You Fat and Thinking Makes You Thin*. She snacks on carrot sticks dipped in low-fat Ranch dressing.

"Can I have a couple?" I ask. I pour a cup of coffee and sit across from her.

"I'll make you a real breakfast," Betty says. She clutches the edge of table and tries to stand. She's been promising breakfast for months.

"Don't worry," I say. "I'll stop at McDonald's on the way to work."

Betty puts her face in her hands and sobs, making her throat skin ripple like the sail on a pirate ship. I reach toward her. My fingers tap the table at the edge of her wrist. "I shouldn't have said that," I say.

Betty quit cooking six months ago when she struck 550 pounds. The only time she leaves the bedroom is early morning, to sit at the kitchen table and pretend she's preparing for an active day. Then I help her back to bed before I go to work, but I'm not a big man. It's getting harder to move her.

In high school, I was one of those narrow-bodied Atari-playing nerds with black-rimmed glasses. The summer after I graduated, I met Betty at the Renaissance Festival and we learned that we were both going to the same college. Before Betty got huge, she was hefty in a bawdy, Bette Midler sort of way, with thick, fluffy boobs that rode high in old-time girdles. I, on the other hand, was diminutive and loved lounge-style singers like Engelbert Humperdinck and Bob Goulet, both of whom once displayed outstanding moustaches. I had a fantastic moustache, too, at the time, a "glue-on" for my Medieval costume, a fluffy red one about half the size of my face. Betty and I were both dressed in period outfits. She strolled through the crowds performing as a mouthy prostitute reciting dirty limericks. Sixteenth-century men appreciated fat hookers. I, on the other hand, was the king's courier because I put little weight on a horse. I wore a green vest, and underneath, a white shirt with puffy arms. Green tights covered my legs. Betty and I danced for the first time at a closing cast member party in the parking lot. When Betty pulled me into her body, my face wedged between her boobs, and I almost suffocated. The prostitute engulfed me, and I was in love whether I liked it or not.

I stop every morning at McDonald's to eat and read the newspaper headlines, and this morning is no different. I bite into a bacon, egg and cheese biscuit and see a story titled *Enge's son Injured in Bonfire Horror* that starts, "The son of singer Engelbert Humperdinck was engulfed in flames as he tended to a bonfire on the grounds of the family mansion." I sip coffee. I love newspaper headlines, but prefer to imagine the stories rather than read them. This may not sound overly stimulating, but it beats lingering at home and hoisting around my wife's bedpan.

When I finish my hash brown patty, I place a lid on

my coffee and walk out to the minivan. On the freeway drive to downtown, I stomp the brakes at 65 miles per hour and then ease up before I spin out. "Shit," I say and accelerate to get back up to speed. "I forgot about Betty."

A truck swerves around me and then slows to get even. The driver gives me the finger.

I forgot to move Betty back to the bedroom, and she couldn't remind me because she was bawling with her face buried in her arms when I left. She'd probably be there all day folded over the kitchen table like a pot roast, unable to reach the phone, sitting in sweet-smelling urine. Betty has diabetes.

Then my cell phone rings and it's my mom, Gail, telling me my dad's in the hospital, but I know this. Chester's been in the hospital for three days. "I'm at the hospital right now, Byron. Get over here now. I'm calling everybody." An orange sign in the shape of a diamond says that freeway construction starts next Monday, so I'll need to find an alternate route.

Chester was mowing the lawn a week ago when his stomach started to pang, but instead of getting off the mower, he waited until the ache got so bad that he grabbed his belly with both hands and drove the tractor into the deck. He tumbled and broke three ribs against the retaining wall at the edge of the deck where Mom had her perennials. His stomach hurts because his liver is rotting.

"Mom, I left Betty at the kitchen table and I have to be at work in ten minutes."

"Get over here and see your father. He's going into septic shock."

"How's Betty going to get to the bedroom?"

"Your father's dying."

"Betty's stuck in the kitchen."

"Isn't there some neighbors you can call?"

"All the guys are at work."

When I was nine, I dropped a lit book of matches on a stack of Chester's work shirts. Gail ran into the living room where she had the shirts folded on the coffee table. She grabbed me by the arm, and I pulled away and laughed at her. Her mouth twisted and eyes watered, and then Chester got home from work. The door banged and when he smelled the burning fibers, he punched me in the mandible. I had my jaw wired shut and the story Gail told the doctor and that I went along with because I couldn't talk anyway was that I got elbowed while playing basketball in the cul de sac, even though I never played basketball in the cul de sac.

The phrase "kids are cruel" is not an empty cliché. The last time I wheeled Betty outside was a year ago for the National Night Out block party in the cul de sac, and the neighborhood moms bent down and patted her puffy hands. Betty smiled back, oxygen tubes roping from her nose like snot strings. Betty uses the air tubes during the day and an industrial-strength breathing machine at night that slams oxygen into her lungs like an air compressor with enough force to blast the stain off of a fence.

On Friday nights, the neighborhood teens not old

enough to drive sneak down to our house at the end of the cul de sac. They want a peek at the mysterious fat lady who hasn't been outside for a year except for the two times she got stretchered to the hospital and one of the kids videotaped the paramedics hauling Betty down the sidewalk on a reinforced gurney that looked like one of those huge-wheeled boat cranes that lifted yachts in and out of the water at marinas. They probably have her on Youtube but I haven't had the courage to search.

I can hear the kids prowling the backyard, even over the hiss and suck of the breathing machine. They sneak into the yard by hopping the fence and try to peer through the lower-level living room windows, hoping to snare a sight, but I keep her bedroom drapes closed, and they can't see me in the dark sitting on the couch. I can see them, though, as they whisper through the yard. They breathe like Betty breathes, hard and deliberate like they mean business, and all I do is watch them. I should yell at them, shout something like "How dare you" or "You should be ashamed of yourself," but I don't. Sometimes I imagine a news story about some teens found dead in a suburban yard while trying to view an obese woman, and there's a mug-shot of me over the shoulder of the news anchor, but instead of a stone face, I'm winking and holding a microphone and my mouth is open as if I'm just about to start singing "Please release me, let me go."

As I sit in the dark, Betty will yell, "Byron, get me cake, goddamnit!" I'm on doctor's orders not to give her cake because of the diabetes. You could make a batch of Krispy Kreme donuts from Betty's blood.

I'll walk into her room, into the tragic stink.

"You file the papers yet?" she'll ask. She always asks the question about the year-old lawsuit that I've never filed on her behalf, but I always say, "Yeah, we should hear from the lawyers soon," and then put a handkerchief over my nose.

"We need to hurt those bastards," Betty says in gurgling breath.

"Definitely," I say. "I'm going to prick your finger now, Honey."

Betty's outburst makes her tired and she closes her eyes as I shove the spring-loaded blood lancet into the side of her middle finger at max pressure because her fingers are calloused from blood tests. They look like sausage links cooked on a George Foreman grill. Why the neighborhood kids would want to look at this is beyond my understanding.

When I walk into my company's offices, I pass the reception desk and enter the staging area that leads to the cubicle complex. It's a small break room the managers frequent. Against one wall stands a refrigerator, sink and countertop with a coffee pot and toaster, and against the other wall are four tables.

"How you doin', Byron," says Dale, a colleague sitting at one of the tables. He's stirring coffee with a swizzle stick.

"Good," I say. "Where'd you get the swizzle stick?"

"What?"

"I need to think for a second."

"Why?"

"My dad's in the hospital."

"Why? What happened?"

"He cracked some ribs."

I walk to my cube and sit in my swivel chair. I grab the bottom of the chair with both hands and kick my heels into the carpet and spin around fast until the cubicle walls pasted with photo-copied jokes blur like a midway carnival seen from a Tilt-a-Whirl. Then I stop spinning and call home, hoping Betty can reach the phone. After two rings, I hang up, realizing she might try to reach the wall phone above the kitchen light switch and fall on the linoleum.

"You should go to the hospital," says Dale, leaning against my cubicle entrance and stirring his coffee.

"Or I could go home first."

"Why?"

"I left Betty at the kitchen table."

"Can't you call somebody?"

"All the neighbor guys are at work."

"What about a moving company?" Dale says. Then he says, "Just kidding, Byron. I'm just flipping you shit." He yawns and walks away.

I log into my computer and click on my desktop link to Engelbert Humperdinck's website to find why his son was having a bonfire. My guess is that he was trying to impress some "birds" he'd picked up at a "pub" by having a party at Enge's estate. All he needed to say was, "My dad is Engelbert Humperdinck" and even though The Enge is seventy, the ladies would swoon, but then what happened is that Enge's son took the birds back to the mansion and became intoxicated on scotch whiskey and fell into the bonfire, or else one of the birds shoved him in when he said something like, "You're just too good to be true, can't take my eyes off of you" and groped her, but then I find the real story: The Enge's daughter writes a poem on the website that says he was helping his mom burn leaves and the winds shifted and "flames engulfed him/ and he had nowhere to run/ except back into the fire/ to pull the tractor out the way/…a stupidly civilized…thinking of the neighbours….heroic move to make/ He then ran to find my mother/ To have her hose him down."

Heroic.

Some might think cynically, however, 1) Why did Enge's son have a tractor parked in a pile of burning lawn rubbish? But the provocative element is this: 2) He was selflessly helping his mom, and 3) He ran to his mom for comfort, which 4) Shows he loves his mother very much, just as I love my mother very much, even though I probably would have let the tractor explode because I'm a coward.

"Byron," says a voice from behind. "If you've got stuff going on, don't worry about sticking around." It's Dale again, yawning.

"I'm pretty busy."

"What are you doing?"

"Solving the Enge mystery."

"You should go move your wife."

"I think she'll be okay."

"Don't you have a nurse or someone you can call?"

"They're pretty busy."

I stay at work until 5:30 and climb into my minivan in the parking garage. I turn on my cell phone and it beeps to indicate a message. It's Gail again: "I need you to get here, Byron. Your sisters are flying in today. I am not kidding around."

I decide to stop home first and help Betty back to bed.

Last night as usual when I got home from work around six, I'd slouched into Betty's room and kissed her pasty forehead, pasty because she sweated prescription drugs through her skull. I also injected chemicals into her body every day and filled her with pills and food. She ate too much sugar and always yelled from the bedroom, "Bring me cake, Byron, goddamnit!"

"Hi, Sweetie," I'd said, leaning over the sweat-soaked bed to kiss her forehead. Chemicals had bloated her face and turned her lips blue. Her eyes looked like soap-filled bubbles. A shoe box full of pill bottles sat on the nightstand on top of a pile of *Star* newspapers.

"Get me cake," Betty had slurred.

"You can't have cake today," I'd said.

"Get me cake, goddamn it!"

So I'd walked into the kitchen, opened the freezer and sawed off a small slab of Sarah Lee frozen pie and brought it to her even though I wasn't supposed to. Then I pressed the button to raise the back of the bed so Betty could eat and squint at the TV.

"Million bucks," she said.

"What, honey?"

"Howie, goddamnit." She'd been breathing fast. "That Mandel guy." Then she'd closed her eyes and snored so I shut off the TV and switched on the breathing machine after attaching the mask to her face.

"I love you, Betty," I'd said, kissing her forehead. I loaded up a syringe with insulin and crooned one of Enge's masterpieces as I moved the syringe toward the halo of needle bruises that circled the sinkhole of her belly button:

> *So I sing you to sleep after the lovin'*
> *I brush back the hair from your eyes.*
> *and the love on your face*
> *is so real that it makes me want to cry.*

Thirty years ago when I was seven, I met The Enge for the first time, and a decade later, met him again when I worked at on the State Fair's Maintenance Crew. Now, exactly twenty years later, as my dad is dying, Enge's 31-year-old son burns himself up at his father's mansion. It's weird how things are connected, whereas at other times, things aren't.

Betty starts to throw off a stink around lunchtime every day. Three years ago, when she was ambulatory, I got her a job at my document production company. Since Betty had an English degree and had taught middle school for three years before her weight started to balloon, she qualified to be a document proofreader.

One morning as I wheeled Betty in, the proofreading

supervisor, a twenty-five-year-old named Norman, shot out from his office and walked alongside us.

"And how are you two today?"

"Good," I said.

"Can you two come into the conference room for a second for a chit-chat real quick?"

I wheeled Betty up to the table, and then Norman and I sat down.

"Betty," said Norman, "We have a special room for you where I think you'll be a lot more comfortable."

"Why?" She breathed fast. "I'm okay where I am."

"We just thought maybe you'd be comfortable with more space."

"What do you mean?"

"A larger table, I mean."

Normally, proofreaders sat in a room with rows of computers facing into each wall, and in the middle of the room were two tables where Norman pulled documents from the printers and checked them for accuracy.

"So," said Betty, fighting for breath, "this means everyone gets a larger table, right, and their own room?"

"We don't have that much space."

"Why just me, Norman?"

Norman cleared his throat. "It's a concern." Norman was a high school substitute English teacher who worked as evening shift supervisor. "About noon every day, the room starts to take on an odor, to be quite honest, and many of the scorers are concerned by this gas."

"What do you mean *gas*?"

"I suppose it's a form of emanation what I'm talking

about, but I would describe it more as a sort of permeation, if you will." Norman's voice softened. "I know this is no one's fault, but it just may be, and I don't know this, but maybe you begin to perspire around that time because of all the work your heart probably has to accomplish. I'm not saying you can help it, but what I am saying, and I need to be entirely clear about this, is that the smell is distracting numerous proofreaders and it's affecting general accuracy."

"Has anyone else complained?"

"In so many words, in so many terms."

Betty curled up her lips and stared at me. "Are you going to file the lawsuit or am I?"

I smiled at Norman. Betty's neck turned red.

That's the story of the lawsuit that never happened and Betty became a shut-in after that.

Once when I was little, I saw Chester beat the shit out of my mom, and then I started having this dream all the time about my mom getting nailed with snowballs by these redneck guys with ball caps and long hair who in real life would throw snowballs at me and my friend Ryan when we walked home from elementary school. When they weren't throwing snowballs, the guys stood by their garage smoking cigarettes and drinking beer, and then they'd toss the empty cans in the air for their Rottweiler to leap up and clench. Once, we threw snowballs back, but our weak tosses barely cleared the chain-link fence, where the dog would leap up and bite the snowballs into small explosions, and right when I threw one and started to fall forward, an ice-ball struck me in the testicles. I curled into the snow and squinted while the redneck guys laughed.

In the dream, though, the rednecks aimed for my mom, and I didn't stand up for Gail as she got pelted and dropped to her knees and cried out with great drama, "Help me, Byron! Make them stop!" The rednecks laughed, stumbling into the side of the garage. I never stepped in front to shield her. I never took a hit for her, and the recurring dream about Gail in pain has something to do with all this crap about Betty and Chester, and though I'm no psychologist, the time I watched Chester beat the shit out of Gail and didn't interrupt but instead went to my room and watched Enge perform on the *Captain and Tennille Show* is when the dreams started, so it doesn't take a fucking psychiatry degree.

I decide I'd better go to the hospital before I go home to move Betty. It's just a hell of a lot closer to work and why waste all that gas and time coming back. A lady with bluish hair at the front desk tells me, "He's in the Intensive Care Unit."

"Why?" I ask.

"All I know is what the computer says."

She gives me directions and I ride the elevator up seven floors. I walk into the ICU, which in the center has a large nurses' station. The rooms that surround the station hold dying people, all of whom are exposed. Each room has for a wall a pane of plexiglass so that each patient can be viewed at all times from the central area.

I see Chester on display behind glass, his jaundiced eyes staring out over a huge oxygen mask clamped to his face. The air pumps in and sucks out hard. Chester's eyes are wide as he strains to keep up with the violent machine. Minus teeth, Chester's lips fly in and out of his mouth over his gums. He shakes his head and stares off to the left. Then he turns his head to the right. Then he looks straight ahead and makes eye contact with me. He paws and scratches at the sides of the mask, but it's on too tight, clutching his face like an alien creature. I almost ask a nurse if he really needs the air-machine, but they seem busy with other dying people. They're like waitresses with too many tables, so you really can't blame them.

When I walk out, the blue-haired lady at the reception desk says, "That was a quick visit."

I first met Engelbert Humperdinck at the State Fair in 1978 when I was seven. Chester and I sat in the grandstand at the State Fair racetrack and watched stock cars drive clockwise. The noise and the reek of exhaust hurt my head, and Chester chowed bratwursts and drank coffee. He gave me five dollars to walk into the grandstand concession area for a soda. Instead, though, I walked further, to where salesmen sold electric bed massagers, water picks and food slicers. The crowd was huge, and I thought I knew where I was, so I kept walking the aisles between booths until I noticed a man in a blue shirt following me. He wore blue jeans, a jean jacket, had a huge mustache, thick glasses and a baseball hat. He looked like one of those celebrities who disguised himself as a salt-of-the-earth person to go out in public. It was Engelbert Humperdinck, who was performing at the grandstand that evening, though I didn't know about Enge at the time.

So, this guy with a huge moustache and fluffy sideburns tapped me on the shoulder and I turned around. He knelt and said, "Are you lost, little man? Where's your folks?"

"My dad's at the car race."

"I'll walk you back there," he said in a deep, English accent.

"I can go by myself."

"I want you to be safe, little man," he said in a rich, heroic voice, and took my hand. I pulled away and said, "Please release me, let me go."

Actually, I didn't say the "Please release me" part. Enge's greatest hit, "Release Me," was recorded in 1967, more than ten years before I met him for the first time.

I've left the hospital and I'm on my way home to move Betty. I need a haircut first, though, and while getting my hair trimmed at Great Clips, for once I actually say, "Um, yeah, sure," when the hairstylist, after she's done trimming, asks, "You want anything in your hair? You want mousse or gel or anything?" When I was younger, I always said in a macho way, "I'm chemical free," but now I say, "Sure, I've never gelled before." This is a huge step.

A hairstylist across the way, washing a lady's hair, laughs, and she's laughing against me. And I also realize that I drive the same minivan I've driven for five years although my wife is too big to wedge into the back even when I remove the seats. And so while the stylist, Jeanne—I learn her name from her graduation certificate on the mirror—cuts my hair, I tell her about the time I worked at the State Fair when I was seventeen and met Enge for the second time:

"I was working on the maintenance crew and me and my friend were in charge of setting up tables and coolers of beer for a Republican party gathering in the infield of the racetrack, in a big tent right behind the Grandstand Stage where the bands play. You know where that is?"

Jeanne says "No" and slides a number four razor attachment along the side of my head.

"So," I say, "when all the people are eating and drinking, me and my friend Tom sort of hang off to the edges of the tent by where the coolers are, and we take turns sneaking beers. The place we go to slam beers is this cement bunker underneath the huge stage; there's bathrooms down there that the pit crews use during the car races. So I grab a couple cans of Old Style and tuck one under each armpit and head down into the bunker... When I get inside, there's this biker guy standing in front of the bathroom door like a bodyguard, so I freeze with the beer under my pits, and the guy has his arms folded, looking tough, but then he turns to me and says 'How are you today?' in this real effeminate voice, and I say 'Good' and almost start to laugh. So then Engelbert Humperdinck walks out of the bathroom, and as he's walking out, he looks me in the eye and says, 'How you doin'?' No shit. He said that. Then I went in the bathroom and slammed the beers."

"I never heard of him," says Jeanne, who seems to be in her twenties. She has a tongue-ring.

"I didn't know who he was at the time, either," I said. "I found out later when I saw a commercial on late at night for a collection of '70s love songs and this guy named Engelbert Humperdinck was singing "The Last Waltz" and my first thought was, 'Jesus, I met that guy!' And my second thought was, 'I didn't know he was the dude who sang that song.'"

"I never heard that song," Jeanne said.

So, I didn't tell her the whole story the way I just said. I think all I said actually was, "I met Engelbert Humperdinck two times" because Jeanne was a non-chatty stylist, and I couldn't think of anything to say, my dad probably dead and my wife beached in the kitchen, and somewhere in there I started to bawl until I couldn't breathe and Jeanne asked if there was anyone I could call.

I turn into the cul de sac around nine. Betty could be dead, and I know the phone messages from Gail scolding me for leaving the hospital before riding out the deathbed scene will be plentiful. I press the garage door opener button clipped to my sun visor. The door opens like a mouth.

I drive in slowly, riding the brake, and when the door closes behind me, I let the car run for awhile. In my final image, there's this guy in a jean jacket holding a little kid's hand and walking into the sunset, leading him to a land of safety and rest. But instead, I go inside and grab a can of Michelob Light and walk into the living room where Betty is belly-down on the carpeting ten feet from the kitchen table. She breathes in short gasps. I phone 911, wheel out her CPAP machine from the bedroom, hook it up to her head, and kneel by her side, and then I lay back against her like she's a bean bag chair. I look at the sliding glass doors, the curtains open, and wait for the teenagers to show up on Friday night as always. If they get here before the ambulance does, I'm going to let them in.

Model Man

Nancy is in a fetal curl on the kitchen floor as she phones her husband at his office. "I called an ambulance," she says. "My stomach kills."

"Is it on the way?" asks Doug.

"Is *what* on the way?"

"The ambulance."

Nancy is only four months pregnant, so Doug knows there must be trouble. He grabs his laptop as he leaves the office because he has an afternoon deadline to finish a website design for a town home developer. All he needs are pictures of healthy-looking families enjoying their homes. He already has the picture boxes placed; he just needs to insert images.

In the emergency room, an anesthesiologist named Chad, with an acre of chest hair sticking out from the V of his green ER jacket, scribbles forms on a clipboard he rests on the food tray and asks Nancy of medication allergies. Doug stays silent.

"Stadol," Nancy moans from the gurney. She's on her

side, pulling her knees to chest. "It gave me hallucinations when I had Sean. I dreamed I had an alien baby."

"We don't use Stadol," says Chad. Then he barks at the nurse. "Where's the goddamn HD2 form, Candy?"

"The blue one in front of your face," Candy says. Then she yawns.

Nancy's doctor, whose name is Sandra Sanderson but who looks to Doug exactly like a middle-aged Pippi Longstocking, sits on a stool and delivers the pre-op consult. "I make a hole next to the belly button with a laser, drop in a small sack like a marble pouch, cut out the section of the fallopian tube with the hemorrhage, drop it into the bag and haul it up. No big deal." Doug sees black-faced miners with lunch pails and hard hats squinting into daylight. Pippi says the surgery will take an hour. She'll slap on a couple industrial-duty Band-Aids and Doug and Nancy will be out in time to extract their kids from daycare without a late fee.

"What about the baby?" Doug asks.

"This is nothing," Pippi says. "I do this procedure in my sleep."

Doug's jaw clenches. He squeezes Nancy's hand, sending her the message, on Pippi's cue, that the procedure is routine, like clipping toenails or restocking water softener pellets, and when Nancy closes her eyes in pain, Doug looks at Pippi and says, "Smile for the camera."

"Pardon?"

"Nothing," says Doug. "No worries. This is nothing."

"No need to be smart," says Pippi. "You can go to the

waiting room now, Dan."

"It's 'Doug.'"

On the way, Doug peeks into the room adjoining Nancy's. A kid with a wrapped head sits on a gurney and stares up into the fluorescent light. A smaller boy stands by the bed and stares up at his big brother. The family had a car wreck. The mother broke an arm, the little brother earned a fat lip, and the father was merely coined-eyed. He was also an employee for one of Doug's clients, a lumber company. Doug remembers the man's face from when he designed the company website; he chose his photo and a few others from among dozens submitted because the company's marketing department wanted him to show a working-class guy who seemed happily employed and productive. In the photo, the family man who'd just crashed-up his wife and kids runs a band saw and wears yellow-tinted shop goggles.

Couches are always so low in hospital waiting rooms, knees always above thighs. Doug sits with his computer on his lap and scours files, mostly stock digital photos of happy people of various ages, ethnicities and genders in home, office and industrial settings. He's staying busy, searching for photos, anything to keep from reading the pamphlets in the magazine rack: "Praying With Someone Sick," "Letting Tears Bring Healing," "Turning to a Counselor for Hope." A stack of *Guidepost* magazines is splayed across an end table.

A yellow phone hangs on the wall and a sign above it commands, "If the phone is ringing, pick it up." There's no sign saying who might be calling. Maybe Pippi, possibly Jesus, maybe a Domino's driver lost at another hospital.

The phone rings as Doug scans stock pictures of a smiling family enjoying its executive-style home, barbecuing on a deck. One photo shows a blonde mother in a red blouse setting a plate of corn on the cob in front of a blonde boy. The father, back to the camera, tends a grill, blue smoke pluming over his shoulders.

Doug uses these kinds of stock family pictures for corporate websites, especially realty agencies and real estate developers, to show family-friendliness and economic security, but he's never noticed this series of barbecue pictures of the same fake family. The mother smiles and serves food in every photo, and in every photo, the boy looks at the food, which is close to reaching him, but not quite. Doug can't see the man's face in any of the pictures. He's always grilling with his back turned. Doug moves the pictures to trash, freeing up memory. Without the man's face, he's got nothing.

The phone stops ringing, replaced by shuffling feet in the corridor. People walk lightly in hospitals because a hard step might make a surgeon's wrist twitch.

Doug stares over his computer into a globe mirror that reflects three converging corridors and watches two doctors stand and chat. One is Doctor Peña, the ER doctor who'd read Nancy's X-rays before turning her over to Pippi for surgery. He's spooning a milkshake out of a styrofoam cup while another doctor with a clipboard says, "How's emergency today?"

"Three car crashes and so forth," says Peña. He squints

and slams his palm into his forehead. "Jesus. I got a brain freeze."

"Ipsilateral orbital?"

"Ouch," says Peña.

Doug closes his computer, pinches his thumb and says, "Fuck." Peña squeezes the skin between his eyes with thumb and forefinger. Doug sucks his thumb, then stands and grabs a *Guideposts* magazine off of the end table by the couch.

He reads an article written by an East Coast trucker who was nervous when freeway snipers were on the loose—they were shooting people in mall parking lots—but then God told him to put out a CB call for all truckers to meet at a rest stop for prayer. A hundred truckers appeared and held hands for an hour, and a week later at another rest stop, the prayer-organizing trucker spotted the suspects' car. Two guys snoozed inside. The trucker radioed the police and while waiting, blocked the exit ramp with his rig.

The trucker's implied argument was that mass-prayer led to capture, even though the other truckers who he prayed with were not on hand when he spotted the sniper, but the trucker missed the real supernatural scheme, that God made him drink an extra cup of coffee at dinner so he had to urinate at the Mile 142 rest area rather than his usual stop further up the turnpike. If he hadn't had one more coffee, more shoppers would have been shot. God created the bladder-pain to save consumers, and then had the trucker write the account so that a middle-aged web designer would be guided by God to read it while his wife's body was being invaded, in order for him to realize that full bladders, fallopian hemorrhages, ice cream headaches and pinched thumbs are messages from on high.

Doug pokes his head into the corridor and says to the chatting doctors, "I'm going to hell."

"How do you know?" says Doctor Peña, massaging the bridge of his nose. "Everything okay, Dan?"

"No worries," says Doug. "This is nothing."

He pulls his head back into the waiting room, and when the phone rings again, he picks it up and drops it, to let it dangle on the yellow cord. It taps against the wall. Moments later, Candy the nurse walks into the waiting room and says to Doug, "I just called. Does the phone work in here?"

"I couldn't answer it," Doug says.

"It's off the hook."

"I was too nervous to answer it. I thought it might be for me."

"It *was* for you. You can go in and see your wife now."

"Is she okay?"

"Everything is fine."

"Is the baby okay?"

"I can't say anything about specifics. The doctor will be in to talk to you about all that."

Nancy is groggy but awake, and sort of waves at Doug when he walks into the room. All of the lights are off except for a small one over a mirror above a cabinet. Doug sits down in a chair between the window and the bed.

"Did the doctors tell you anything?" she asks, her voice hoarse and sexy like when they were in their early twenties and waking up with hangovers in tents.

"Nothing," Doug says. "I only talked to that one nurse."

"What'd she say?"

"She wondered why I didn't answer the phone."

"What?"

"Did the doctors talk to you?" he asks.

"Just real quick. I lost the baby but they said there's more."

"What more?" says Doug.

"At least we have Sean and Amber," she says, reaching out and gripping Doug's hand hard. He pulls back, thinking this is too much like a scene in a Sunday Night Movie. Nancy never usually expresses emotion like on television, so he chalks it up to the pain medications.

"It's okay," he says. "Sean and Amber are plenty enough to deal with anyway."

"What do you mean by that?" Her grip tightens.

"I'm trying to be jokey."

She releases his hand, shuts her eyes, and opens and closes her mouth the way they used to do when they were stoned and had cotton-mouth. A thin white string of dried saliva circles her lips like clown make-up.

"You want some ice in a cup or something?" he says.

Doug walks out in the brightly lit hallway while Nancy rests. He finds an ice and water machine along a wall, and next to it, a coffee pot. He fills her cup of ice water and himself a foam cup of burned coffee and turns around. Blocking his path to the room is Dr. Peña, the emergency room doctor with the ice cream headache.

"How's the wife?" he says.

"She's groggy but still alive."

"That's what I like to hear, Champ," he says. He walks off, but before doing so, pats Doug on his left shoulder, like a buddy.

Nancy is snoring when the doctor who looks like Pippi Longstocking walks in and stands next to her, opposite the side of the bed where Doug sits and sips coffee.

"We met before surgery," she says to Doug, smiling with her teeth but not her eyes. "I'm Sandra Sanderson." She looks to Doug like the precocious storybook girl who in his youth outwitted pirates, only she's now older and more in need of sleep. She wears the typical blue baggy pants and v-neck shirt of surgeons everywhere.

"We have the same kinds of names," Doug says.

"Sanderson?"

"No, first names like our last names. My last name is Douglas and my first name is Doug. Doug Douglas. And you're Sandra Sanderson."

"I see," she says.

"My biological dad's name was 'Pilquist,'" says Doug. He doesn't want Pippi to talk about his wife yet. He's not ready. Pippi's face looks stern. "But when my mom remarried, she made me take the new guy's name."

"Very interesting," Pippi says.

"She wanted family unity and all that, never mind

that I got made fun of."

"Understandable," says Pippi. "Now onto the business at hand."

"When my teachers took roll," Doug says, "they said 'Douglas Douglas,' and I could hardly say 'here' because the class was laughing." Caffeine charges through his nervous system. He wonders if caffeine actually goes into the nerves. And he also wonders if the doctor might be the 'real' Pippi Longstocking from the old movies. He wants to ask her.

"Anyhow," says Pippi, "since your wife seems to be sleeping, you and I can talk."

Nancy lifts her head. "I'm up," she says.

Pippi reaches down and pats Nancy's right hand. "We can all talk, then." She then puts both hands on the bed rail like a cow farmer grabbing a fence, and looks at Doug. "We lost your baby," she says. "The baby was stillborn, and what we initially thought was hemorrhage wasn't what we thought it was. This is the tough part."

"What is?" says Doug.

"Having to tell patients not-the-best-news. That's the tough part of this job."

"I mean what did you find in there? What things?" Doug says. Nancy's eyes are closed again.

"We found a tumor on one of Nancy's fallopian tubes." Doctor Pippi reaches over the rail and strokes Nancy's hand again and narrows her eyebrows into a practiced squint like the face a news anchor wears during the transition from a story about a little boy who has beaten cancer because of the money raised by a neighborhood fundraiser to a story about a murder-suicide in a suburb. "We tried to remove all of it, but only time can tell. The more major concern is that there was also a small tumor attached to the pancreas, which is double trouble."

"Like that Elvis movie?" says Doug.

"I don't know about that," says Doctor Sanderson. "But I need you to know that if we're dealing with pancreatic cancer, we're dealing with a most serious kind. Still, we haven't got the results back from the biopsy of either tumor yet, so it's tough to say anything for certain right now. We'll know more when both are analyzed."

"When will we know?"

"Later tonight or tomorrow morning."

Doug looks at his watch. It says it's quarter-to-five p.m. Nancy groans, her eyes batting open and then closing. Doug feels a knot in his stomach, knowing he'll have to repeat all of this to her when she's awake. Plus, he has to pick up Sean and Amber at daycare by six. He'd already emailed his brother Dale to be ready to pick them up if he couldn't. And he needs to figure out a way to ask this doctor if she is in fact the child actor who played Pippi Longstocking.

"What if the tumors are malignant?" Doug asks.

"Then we'll need some aggressive treatment, Dan."

"Doug."

"Doug, we're going to move you folks over to an oncologist to take over the care from here." She reaches down and pats Nancy's right hand again. "Any other questions for me before I go?"

Doug, knowing this may be the last time he will see

Pippi, says, "You look like a girl who I saw played on TV back when I was a kid."

"Laura from *Little House on the Prairie*?" Dr. Sanderson says, raising the left corner of her mouth, almost smiling. "Melissa Gilbert?"

"I was actually thinking of someone else."

"I appreciate it when people make that comparison," the doctor says, "because Melissa Gilbert has done a lot of real-life work for the church, which is admirable. I try to do much for my church as well."

Doctor Pippi stands silent, hands gripped to the bed rails, and fixes Doug in the eyes.

"Okay," Doug says. "That sounds good." And he thinks of the *Guideposts* article about the prayer-group sniper-spotting trucker and wonders, even though Nancy is the one in pain, if he's getting hit with some sort of divine message, and that maybe prayer is the only way to dry up Nancy's tumors. "Are you saying this is pretty serious then?" he says, his voice shaking. "Are you saying we should pray?"

Dr. Sanderson closes her eyes and shakes her head no. "Doctors can't pray with patients," she says. "It's a policy matter. But I can get someone in here for you. We have spiritual consultants on call."

"I'm just asking if it would help."

"We just need to prepare for a smooth landing here," she says, narrowing her eyes again and spinning toward the door like a ballerina who's just finished a dance.

Doug shoulders his laptop bag and walks back to the

waiting room while Nancy sleeps. He sits on the couch and opens his computer to continue to find images of a happy family at the barbecue for the town home developer's website. He had deleted the ones with the man grilling meat with his back turned to the camera and his wife and son grinning at the table behind him. He still needs a man's face.

Then he calls his brother Dale on his cell phone to tell him to go ahead and pick up Amber and Sean from daycare. "We might be here awhile," Doug says. "They want to keep her overnight to take a look at how her tummy is recovering."

"What happened, Doug?"

"She lost the baby and now she's got some tumors, but no worries, Dale. Don't tell the kids yet, buddy. We just have to prepare for a smooth landing here."

"What does that mean?"

"We'll know more later. Thanks for getting the kids, buddy."

Doug hangs up and thinks of the last time him and Nancy were in this same hospital. It wasn't because anyone was dying, but instead because they took Sean, who was only five, shore-fishing at a nearby lake. Doug was in the parking lot digging through the back of the car for folding chairs and Nancy was standing by the beach play area rubbing her newly swelling belly, pregnant at the time with Amber, and talking to another mother who had one hand on a stroller and another hand on her hip. Sean was down at the lakeshore, fishing, standing on a boulder in a row of boulders, all placed there to cut down on beach erosion. Each rock had a kid standing on it.

Then Doug noticed that Sean stepped back off of his rock and dropped his fishing pole and bent over, and the two kids on each side of him stepped back with him. When Doug got to Sean, the boy was holding his cheek with a cupped palm. Doug knelt and pulled away Sean's hand, he saw a jig hook wedged into the lad's skin, and the line from the hook was going into the end of the pole of another kid next to him who was trying to keep slack in the line. The boy beside Sean had cast sideways, at a forty-five degree angle, instead of overhand, and snagged Sean's cheek with his hook.

Doug would have done what any calm person would have done—the same thing his own dad had done when he hooked his boyhood dog through the nose with a spinner lure—gone into his tackle box and pulled out pliers with a wire-cutter and clipped off the end of the hook with the barb on it and then extracted it backwards, but the problem is that the hook went into Sean's cheek sideways and the tip never curled back out, and so the barb was embedded inside the flesh. Aside from the emergency room, Doug's only options were to pull out the hook from the back, thus tearing the flesh with the hook-barb or else pushing the hook all the way through the skin until the barb was out into the air, and then clipping it off with the wire cutters and pulling out the hook from behind. But he would have to break flesh in either direction without any kind of sedative for the boy or himself, and so instead, Doug snapped the fishing line with his teeth and put Sean in the car. Then they all drove to the E.R., the same where he took Nancy, and a doctor shoved a needle into Sean's cheek to numb it, and then wrapped a strip of gauze through the U-end of the hook and yanked before anyone expected it, and the hook extracted into the air with no blood and zero pain. Like magic. But Sean still won't go fishing with Doug. And at no time during the event was there any thought of praying to Jesus. But now is different, a real emergency, and Doug might be raising his kids alone. But he doesn't want to think about that, and instead of going back to work on the website design, the deadline of which he has missed, he instead Googles "Pippi Longstocking" and finds out that the name of the girl who starred in the classic movies was Inger Nilsonn, not even close to Sandra Sanderson—except that her last name is definitely Scandinavian—but the fact that the doctor thought she looked like Melissa Gilbert, who played Laura Ingalls Wilder in *Little House on the Prairie*, makes Doug want to punch something, and the fact that he's also missed his work deadline, can't pick up his kids on time from daycare, and that it sounds like his wife has terminal cancer, makes him realize he is failing at a good clip today, and not because of anything he's done. And that's what pisses him off. He doesn't know what to do: go in and see Nancy, call someone else, finish the website even though he missed the deadline, maybe call his boss and tell him what's going on. Maybe he'll talk to the kids on the phone when they get back to Dale's house. He wants to talk to the kids, but he doesn't want to say anything.

The yellow phone on the wall rings and Doug's stomach feels like an electrical charge. It rings again. He closes his laptop, and instead of answering the phone, reaches to the table at the side of the couch and grabs another *Guideposts*. Instead of opening the magazine, he looks at the cover. He sees the title story on the cover listed as, "A Boy and His Mom: A Picture of Triumph," and the cover picture shows a red-headed mother with hair not like Pippi Longstocking, but thicker, like Pinky Tuscadero from *Happy Days*—the older Tuscadero sister who dated Fonzie, not the younger one, Leather Tuscadero—helping a young boy onto the saddle of a horse, or else helping him off. Doug can't tell whether he's getting on or off. The mother is smiling up at the boy who is on the saddle, leaning forward toward the mother's hands, which he still grips, right above the knob where the reins go around.

Doug thinks the boy might be blind because he has a vacant stare and a stiff face, but he's in profile, so it's hard to tell. The boy wears a red flannel shirt like Howdy Doody, who was Richie Cunningham's hero on *Happy Days*, and jeans and a cute black cowboy hat with a feather in it, but Doug doesn't think the kid looks happy to be on the cover of a nationally-known Christian inspirational magazine headed by Norman Vincent Peale, the guy who wrote *The Power of Positive Thinking*.

Doug opens the magazine up to the lead story and it shows another picture, this time of the mother on the horse, holding the reins, and the boy on the front of the saddle between her legs, still looking downward with a serious stare. The mother still smiles, but this time into the camera. And now the article title is different from on the cover. The title is "A World of Hope and Beauty," and the mother is the writer of the story, which tells that her son was born too early and came out at two pounds, which is probably about what Doug and Nancy's own baby weighed this afternoon when the doctors extracted it from her. The red-headed mother and her husband looked at their pale, fist-sized baby sucking on a ventilator, and the husband said to the wife, "We need to have hope. We can endure if we have hope." Doug never knew anyone who used the word "endure" in conversation, just politicians and administrative types who gave "addresses" to large audiences.

On top of the kid being born too early, the boy had toxoplasmosis, which can cause blindness. Gary's fingers make the magazine pages quiver. And the boy's heart went into failure and got restarted, but then the next day a doctor told them the boy would always be blind. The mother and father went home that night and couldn't sleep, so instead they prayed and heard a voice that said, "Surrender him to me."

It's not clear whether the wife and husband both heard the exact phrase at the same time, but nonetheless, the boy improved. He started breathing without a ventilator and plumped up, but he was still blind, which couldn't be fixed like in old times when Jesus was in man form and curing retinal damage with swipes of his palms on faces. So the end result was that the parents felt blessed that their boy had survived, but in the photographs, to Doug at least, the boy looks pissed off, and nowhere in the story does the boy get to tell how he feels. Instead, it's all the mom telling about how she surrendered her life, with the Lord's guidance, and even sacrificed her career as a receptionist at a community college in order to care for the boy round the clock, along with a full-time assistant they hired.

And then Doug has a realization: no one ever asks him how he feels about anything, either. It's just not an expectation. He hears a lot of the "How are you today?" and "How's it going?" phrases, but that's just chit-chat from acquaintances and retail clerks. No one has ever asked him how he's *felt*, though, and meant it, except for Nancy a couple times, and then he only got pissed off. He's got feelings but can't figure a way to express them without seeming like a cry-baby.

And the story gets worse, as inspirational stories usually do: the boy goes deaf. He not only can't see, but now he can't hear, and the only way he can communicate is through feeling fingertips bump onto the palms of his hands in regular sequences.

"Holy fuck," Doug says out loud, and wonders how a deaf and blind person could kill himself, not knowing what a gun is, how to find one, or load it, or shoot it, or even what sleeping pills were, where they were stored, or how to find them and take the cap off the bottle. The boy was in constant darkness and silence, and worse, had no way to end his life without making a bloody mess because a mother or a nanny always had their eyes on him even though he could only sense the world by what touched his skin. *Surrender him to the Lord*, thinks Doug. And he thinks about how Nancy is soon going to be blind and deaf, but at least she won't be alive to feel it, and once Doug has this thought, he feels like shit about having it.

There's still no one in the waiting room, just Doug and the magazines and the phone hanging on the wall.

At the end of the article, there is a photo of the family around a grand piano and there's a dark-haired father and the red-haired mother and three other kids, not including the blind and deaf boy. One child is a teenage girl standing near the piano—at the right side of the photo—and she holds the blind and deaf boy. She is smiling. The boy, who must be six or seven, is curled in her arms in a fetal ball, unsmiling, his cowboy hat nowhere in sight. Everyone else in the family is smiling and well-dressed, including a couple of newer toddlers.

To Doug, everything the mother wrote, like, "Just when I thought I would never be able to communicate with my blind/deaf son and make him understand that I love him, today when I sign the words 'I love you' across his chest, his face lights up," doesn't hide the fact that the boy's face tells an opposite story. And Doug realizes he needs to get back to work and get his images for the website but the nurse Candy walks into the waiting room. Doug looks up over the top of the magazine at her and he's got hot tears dumping from his eyes and he can't help it. He's not sure why he's crying but he feels like he felt when he got busted by his mother while jerking off to a *Penthouse* in his back garage when he was thirteen.

"Sorry," he says, putting the magazine down on his

computer keyboard on his lap.

"I tried calling again," Candy says. "I figured you were in here and I don't have your cell number." She moves back a step when she notices Doug's smeared eyes. "Everything is fine," she says. "No worries. The oncologist just wants to talk to you and your wife."

Doug thinks he's supposed to ask her to pray with him—then he could have his own little hope anecdote to send into *Guideposts*—to see if anything happens, but he knows she'll just say what Pippi said: "I can't pray with patients. It's policy. I can call in a pastor or something, though." And he's not sure if he's supposed to be piecing together a set of divine messages here, messages that when combined will add up to one big and clear message like the truck driver got, or the message that the husband and wife of the blind/deaf kid got, in actual English dialogue from on high:

Surrender him to me.

Doug Douglas, however, isn't getting a message. Somewhere down the line, his inability to connect with spirits must mean he's inherently fucked up. But he can't figure out why. He's tried praying hundreds of times in good faith effort, and he's only gotten dial tones in return, so to speak. So maybe it's the Lord who's being the prick. So Doug concludes that either the Lord is a prick, or there is no Lord at all, because Doug has been working his ass off to be a good guy. But now his wife might be dying and he's got to step it up even more. That's the real picture he's dealing with. And so he has a sort of epiphany: the pain he feels in his own gut is either something to do with the caffeine, or the stress of realizing that if it's not snipers or blindness stealing your children, it's cancer coming to snipe your wife, and there's not a fucking thing a guy can do about any of it except to drop to his knees and pray, to pretend like someone or something that gives a shit is on the other end of the line, to pretend anything, like you did when you were a kid until the pretending seems real, because without that, all you've got for comfort is what's in front of your face, which is why Doug rubs his eyes clean and pops back open his laptop to retrieve the photos from the trash of the man who grills corn, his back turned to the camera, and the wife and little boy who smile over food.

Animals in Distress

Warm blood drains through my teeth. I sit on my haunches in tall grass, chomping until I nibble bone and become sleepy. Low fall clouds skate across the sky.

"Fox," I say. "Tasty."

An elbow bangs my ribs. I roll to my side and meet my wife's sleep-swelled cheeks. Moonlight flows through the window and fills the wrinkles that carve the outer edges of Verona's eyes.

"You're talking in your sleep," she whispers. "You said 'fox.'"

"Tasty fox," I correct, and close my lids, which scrape dry eyeballs.

"What are you dreaming about?" she says.

I'm dreaming some wild shit.

When I wake, I shower but don't wash my hair. Not that I have much to fuss over; I'm bald but for a thin swath of gray fuzz around the sides and back, and my mouth is filled with a fabricated set of flattened grinders stained yellow from coffee brewed in a state-owned percolator, a rotund metal vat that uses two pre-filled, air-sealed packages of grains per 40-cup fill.

I peer in the mirror, Colgate tube limp in my hand, and rope my tongue around my gums and cheeks, lapping the remnant juices of blood and salt. In my dream, I have sharp teeth. I kill with them and rip at tough, fibrous meat.

I walk to the kitchen and kiss the wife as she labors over the stove, working eggs and sausage links for the grandkids. Carl Jr. and Kenny bounce in their chairs and poke at their empty plates. Jennifer sleeps with her head on a Snoopy placemat. I never respected Snoopy. Admired for his puckishness, the dog is pure laziness, round belly swelled with sloth and indolence, dependent on the feedings of others, instincts dulled by a full dog dish.

"Put that little spoiled mutt in the woods on his own," I'd once told Verona, "and see what *that* teaches America's youth." Red stains on white fur. I smiled.

"Grandpa," Kenny yells, with no intention of making a point. Spurred by his noise, Carl Jr. grunts and bangs silverware. "Wake up, darling," I say to Jennifer, squeezing the back of her neck. Her blue eyes peel open. She frowns at my smile, the unshaven face, yellowing teeth.

"Where's your suit coat, Doctor?" Verona says.

My wife, who taught junior high school for thirty years, backs her elbows in and out over the stove. She wears a housedress of bloated orange flowers over a blue background, her hair a gray bundle compressed under a black hairnet. "Your goddamn eggs are almost ready, boys," she says. Verona's lost her delicacy with kids since she retired.

I wink at Jennifer and she smiles. "Did you dream about the fox, Grandpa?"

The boys laugh.

"Why don't you have your suit on?" Verona says. "You look like shit." She shoves plates of grease-fried eggs in front of the boys. I wear a white dress shirt and slacks, but no tie. "Hygiene is a basic rule in life," she says, for the boys' benefit and my own. "The rest will take care of itself." She's been worried about my condition, thinking that if I simply present myself in a tidier fashion, I'll be okay.

"It's strategy, Vonnie," I say, sliding my plate toward Carl Jr. "Part of the trickiness. Eat my eggs, kid. I'm not into that kind of protein."

"What are you talking about?" Verona snaps. "Why don't you eat your own damn food? Carl can't eat all those eggs."

I lean over to Jennifer and whisper, "I killed a fox last night. I didn't *find* it dead. I killed it."

Jennifer's eyes fly open. "How?" Carl Jr. looks on with a comatose expression.

"I didn't think I had it in me," I say. "I was just starving. I mean, gut-hungry." I rub my lean belly. Jennifer drives her fork into an egg yolk and wrinkles her nose at the creamy bleeding pool. I lean to her ear. "I ate the whole thing. I still taste the blood."

Verona says, "You can't go to work like that, Doctor."

Verona calls me Doctor, like everyone else, because even though I'm a public welfare caseworker who makes a schoolteacher's salary, I have a PhD in Sociology. I'm good support for those who argue against the material value of higher education.

I stand, lick my wife on the forehead, and walk out the door. I see my neighbor Doug ride his ten-speed out of his garage, down his driveway and out into the cul de sac. He rides a bike to his job at some high-tech company in an industrial park. He turns and gives me the thumbs-up sign and yells, "Have a good day, Doctor. Go get 'em."

"Yeah, Doug. Okay."

My neighbor Doug helped start my transformation. He gave me the spark. About a year ago one morning, he peddled past my house so fast that I ran outside to see what was going on. He raced into the cul de sac and turned wide around the circle. He was almost over sideways, leaning deep into the turn like a speed cyclist, and then he straightened up at full sprint and shot onto 152nd, going hard because a coyote was chasing him. I rubbed my eyes like a cartoon character expressing disbelief and walked back into the kitchen where Verona hovered over the stove. Steam rose up over her shoulders like swamp mist.

"What are you doing?" she said. She didn't turn around.

"I just saw Doug peddling his ass off."

"Exercising again?"

"Goddamn coyote's chasing him."

Doug and I are the cul de sac's early risers. Doug gets up early to peddle off the belly he started growing when he turned thirty-five, and I get up early to drive into work and read the news on the Internet before the clients start calling in for their subsistence checks. It's my only downtime in a day spent with the working poor in the city and the ones who live in my basement, my forty-year-old unemployed son Carl, his second wife Janet who works at Walgreens, and their three kids: Kenny, Carl Jr., and Jennifer. Carl and his wife Janet take their meals downstairs—beer, ramen noodles, and dope converted from the subsistence checks I help them draw—but they send the kids up to us to eat. Jennifer is the only kid who doesn't kill me with needs.

When I got to my cubicle that morning after I saw Doug trying to escape the dog, I logged onto the computer. The lead news story was titled, "Coyote Drags Suburban Woman's Yorkie Into Woods." I considered forwarding the story to the cul de sac neighborhood association because our neighbor just got chased by a coyote, so it was relevant and timely, and I'm also the guy who forwards stories to the cul de sac. It's a power I wield carefully, though, so as not to incite hysteria. I forwarded the first stories on deer ticks, encephalitis-spreading mosquitoes, radium in the water supply, the radon gas seeping into houses from the ground, and that flu that seemed to target retarded kids. When I broke the Anthrax threat, everyone in the neighborhood started to sneak up to their mailboxes from behind. When I warned the sac of SARS, Mark and Laura Gustafson canceled their trip to the Yogi Bear campground in International Falls because it was too close to Canada. I also passed on the stories about weird vehicles driven by shadowy figures lurking in neighborhoods and leaving empty bikes lying in streets.

The story's lead photo showed a blonde lady in the yard of her four-story golf course adjacent home. She wore a fantastic smile and cradled her bandaged puppy in red-sweatered arms. "We moved here because of the schools," she said, "but also because our backyard is nature and we're environmentalists. We love to watch the deer eat out of our feeder." She said the Yorkie had limped into the house, a gash on its thigh. "My kids play in this yard. I'm frightened for their safety." She was worried coyotes would start dragging kids away. The final picture showed a wooden play-gym, empty of kids, a green swing hanging motionless in the air at an angle, held up by an invisible breeze.

I used to be afraid for my kid, too. As a baby, Carl stayed up all night crying from the dresser drawer. We couldn't afford a crib since Verona was still in college and I'd just finished my Doctorate and worked janitorial at the University of Washington. I removed the top three drawers so Carl could breathe but not crawl out, but at six months, he clawed his way up and wormed out from the space where the top drawer used to be. He hit the hardwood floor, rolled to his belly and tried to crawl. Blood streamed down the back of his head and over both sides of his neck. He returned from the hospital with staples in his skull.

After he tumbled from the dresser, we put him in a cardboard box on the floor next to another box stuffed with a litter of bald puppies that our collie Lady had dropped. Carl was bedded down like the dogs, except he had blankets underneath him instead of shredded newspapers that reeked of ammonia.

One night, a little stoned, I was washing dishes, Carl behind me on the floor, and I watched the submarines move across the Puget Sound, which was about fifty yards from the kitchen window. The Bangor Navy base housed the Trident Submarine fleet, some of which passed by every night during the ten o'clock news like a conspiracy. I saw the moving lights and felt the rumble of machinery move through the water, onto the land, through the kitchen linoleum and into my feet. The horn from the Hood Canal Bridge sounded like a moose taking a dump.

Carl was in his box next to the puppies. He lay on his belly on the pillow, his back naked and cloth diaper wrapping his ass, cross-hatched black staples on the back of his bald skull. I looked into the dark and then over my shoulder at the dogs and kid whimpering. Verona was off at a night class and I was high and wondering where we'd gotten this baby. Who put those things in the boxes? Should I feed them? What would they smell like dead? Like mice decomposing in walls, huddled up in insulation, the parents having eaten the babies and then gotten too full of them to live? That's how I am forty years later: bloated on kids. Carl won't leave my basement. He's embedded.

As I ride the morning elevator, the steam from my coffee wavers to the intra-office instrumental music of Barry Manilow—*His name was Rico, he wore a diamond*—I think of the elaborateness of my dream. After eating the fox, I feel drunk and on the lip of blackout, muscles numb and brain buzzing like an air compressor. I stand near the edge of a lake, my back and sides itching from sweat. I scratch my left flank with my hind paw and nibble my fur as if trying to extract a burrowing bug. Pinpricks tingle beneath my polyester shirt as I enter the cubicle maze, scratching and humming about Lola being a showgirl.

"Morning, Doctor," says my cubicle partner, Stephan. "Got fleas?"

Stephan clenches a phone in one hand while the other cups the receiver. He can't use the headsets because his sweat pools in the foam earpiece and the foam-free model won't stay affixed in his perspiration stream. His forehead and skull wrinkle from a forced smile, his final smile of the day, energy drained. Stephan's glossy eyeballs tell me he's been up all night drinking scotch again, and sweat circles expand from the furnace of his armpits. A mist generated by his humid forehead smears the upper hemisphere of his black-rimmed glasses.

"You still a dog?" he asks. I hang my trench coat on the rack outside the cubicle wall, signifying I am "in," and drop into my chair to the familiar squeal of ancient spring and metal.

"Why stop now?"

Our personnel director, Patty, a burly state employee who nibbles Sun Chips between sentences, has already confronted me about my canine issue. She said I could take a paid vacation any time. "We owe you, Wesley."

"I want more," I'd said.

"Name it. We value your service."

"A decent supply of meat," I'd said. "And sanctuary."

She wrote that in her report.

"You got messages," Stephan says, lunging into a cough.

I look down at dozens of Post-It notes spread across the desk like dandelions in a meadow of wildflowers: medical reports; memos from Child Welfare Services; grievance letters from landlords, tenants, neighbors, clients, relatives; delinquency notices for electric, cell phone, and cable bills. I pick the desk clean of the yellow squares that order my tasking, crumble them into a tiny balls and toss them into the aluminum waste can that has pressed against my right shin for two decades, creating a horizontal indentation in my bone. I punch off the answering service, strap on my phone headset, lean back and answer the incoming call. "Wesley Boorman, PhD."

"Hey Doctor, this is Annette Anderson." The voice sounds like cigarettes and sick toddlers. "My ex came by and took my check again. I got five kids and gotta feed them somehow and I can't feed them when he keeps taking my checks."

"Is he still threatening you?" I ask. I punch computer keys to call up her report. "You'd better call the police, then, right Annette?"

"So in other words," she says, "I need a new check."

"I'm not sure what I can do if the check has been cashed. The question is, what can *you* do?"

"No disrespect, Doctor, but I don't have time for a moral lesson. I got six mouths to put food into."

The computer screen lists four kids, no spouse; addresses for five relatives, none of whom want contact with Annette.

"Here's what I can do," I say, stumbling on an old trick. "I'm going to send you a form. Your kids need clothes right? Winter's coming. Fill out the form and send it back and I'll send you a stipend for winter clothes."

"They don't need clothes, Doctor. I need money so I can get food." A baby howls. Something smacks a floor.

"Listen, the grant is delivered as a check, Annette. Cash the check."

"This is bullshit."

After she hangs up, I open the file drawer, remove a form and stuff it into an envelope. I throw it in the plastic "Out" tray hanging on the exterior cubicle wall. Someone whose name I don't know but has been saying "Good morning" to me for fifteen years will collect it and take it somewhere else.

Stephan cups his hand over his phone and says, "Lunch?"

"Not hungry," I say, rubbing my gaunt belly. Plus, it's only ten a.m. Stephan and I have eaten chicken fried steak daily for the last decade, but fat never sticks to me. I'm lanky, all bone.

I click the phone back on.

"Doctor, this is Wayne Marshall. I still can't find work and I lost my damn check again and my kid just got diagnosed with a little cancer. How you doing today?"

As I retrieve Wayne's file, I stare at Stephan, the back of his hair soaked in sweat. After I'd finished scratching my moist flank, I'd run through the woods, looking for the den, but forgot where it was. Coyotes weren't supposed to get lost.

I hang up the phone and say, "I have to reposition myself. My nature is dulled."

Stephan squints, and I stalk to the elevator, fluorescent lights digging into the back of my neck. I still itch.

"The goddamn garage door is busted," Verona says when she walks in the front door. I'd just gotten home after work and threw my briefcase on the couch, sat down at the kitchen table to a quiet house, for once—the grandkids in the basement, Carl and Janet at their counseling session, part of Carl's rehab after his third DWI—and Verona had been volunteering at the grade school, making stage decorations for a musical where the kids sang songs about springtime from different cultures around the world as part of the school's diversity effort.

"Maybe the remote batteries are dead," I say.

"I can see the light come on in the garage, so it's getting a signal."

"Maybe it's jammed."

"No shit it's jammed," Verona says, unpacking groceries onto the counter. "Take care of it."

Hearing our footsteps, Carl Jr. and Kenny run up the steps. Carl Jr. yells, "I'm hungry." Carl is nine and tall with a long face that sags like a beagle's. "Crackers," Kenny says. Kenny is six and has a permanent ring of dirt around his mouth. Both kids have uncombed brown hair down to their shoulders. "I mean a popsicle," Kenny says,

"I'm hungry."

Verona sighs and says, "Learn how to ask nice and quit being little shits." I open the freezer for the box of sugar-free popsicles and then the cabinet for the crackers, which I pour into a Tupperware container for Carl Jr. to take downstairs and spill and crush into the carpet. Verona walks into the bedroom to get her sweater. Since she retired, she's been wearing old-lady sweaters, light blue with puffy little flowers on them, and I want to yell, "Jesus, Vonnie, why do you have to act your age?"

After dinner—macaroni and cheese for the kids and pork chops for us—I get an email from Carl. "Dad," it says, "me and Janet are moving out ttyl." Even though he lives in the basement, Carl emails me. He's always on the computer playing games where he pretends to be a knight or a Trojan warrior. Normally, Carl and his wife moving out would make happy, but he says later in the email that they aren't taking the kids with them, and their counselor "gave us the legal surrender paperwork to look over," as though I don't know the paperwork. My office cabinet is filled with surrender paperwork.

I walk across the kitchen, open the basement door and walk downstairs.

"What's the occasion?" says Carl. He glances at me from his computer, which sits on a cluttered stand next to the kitchen bar area. Carl wears white BVD underwear and a black t-shirt that says *Linkin Park*. Carl Jr. and Kenny jump on a red leather couch like they're doing aerobics and watch a *Road Runner* cartoon, which makes my hands tremble so much that I ball them into fists.

"Why are you watching that crap?" I ask.

"It's funny!" Carl Jr. screams.

Jennifer walks out of the bedroom holding a clear container with dirt in it, some kind of bug-catcher. "I'm going over to Kaylee's house to do science homework."

"I'm in the middle of this game," says Carl. "Hang on a second."

"What?" says Jennifer, surprised Carl said something. She stands still.

"I got your email," I say.

"Oh yeah, I have all the paperwork here somewhere." Carl swivels in his office chair and looks at a table cluttered with papers, clothes, cups, dishes, computer manuals. He sighs and swivels back around to the computer screen. "I'll be done in just a sec."

"Janet working tonight?" I ask.

"She's always working, man," Carl says, suddenly tapping the space bar really fast. "Fuck. Ugh."

"At least one of you is working," I want to say, but then I see the cartoon coyote swallow a bottle of leg-growth pills and his bony legs bulk up like a bodybuilder's and start to churn at high speed until they're a round blur of energy and he zips down the road and flies past the bird and goes straight off a cliff, keeps running over the canyon and smashes into the other side. Then he pauses, smashed into the rock, and looks directly at the audience with chagrin before he slides down and out of the picture.

"What an idiot!" Carl Jr. screams.

"Don't say 'idiot'," Carl says. Then he looks at me and shakes his head. "I don't know how to control these kids, man. You see that shit?"

"Then get off the computer," I say. "Put on some pants."

"Yeah right," Carl says with mock sarcasm. "Like that's gonna happen." Carl knows how to play the self-pity off me and everyone. *I fell on my head when I was a baby. I got a TBI. Traumatic Brain Injury. All that helps me is weed and LCD screens, man. No shit. The waves are soothing, man.* Carl weighs two hundred sixty pounds. His furry belly protrudes from under his t-shirt. He has thick black hair that reaches his shoulders and he's bald on top.

"We're not having a talk," I say. "I'm just saying no. It's not going to happen."

"Thermopylae, I rule you!" Carl yells and pumps his fist at the computer screen, and this gets Carl Jr. and Kenny jumping even harder on the couch and Kenny yells, "Wile E. Coyote, I rule you!"

Jennifer, cheeks red, walks upstairs with her bug catcher and I follow her. At the top of the stairs, I close the door. Jennifer turns to me and says, "You just have to ignore them more."

"Ignore your father?" I say. "Is that okay?"

"It just is," she says. Then she walks out the front door and I walk out onto the back patio.

"We can work this out," Carl says to me. I don't turn around to see if he's put on any pants. I stare into the woods and wetland that touches the back of our property. "We can't take care of the kids, man. We're just not natural parents."

I want to say, "You make your bed," or something like it, but I can't. It's like a bone is wedged in my esophagus. I want to tell Carl that I'm old and tired and want to be alone for awhile before I croak, that I'd been doing nothing but feeding people all my life, but instead I spin around and growl. Carl's eyebrows come together to form one large one. He squints and cocks his head at me like a small dog who's just heard something strange.

After my neighbor Doug got chased by the coyote, I had to ask him about it. I walked across the lawn over to his patio where he was having a cigarette and a beer before bedtime.

"You saw it, Doctor? Will you tell my wife? She thinks I'm shitting her."

"Vonnie thought I was bullshitting, too."

"Jesus," he said, staring into the wetlands at the backs of our properties. "I couldn't believe it."

"You read the article I emailed?"

"I haven't been on the computer all day. I didn't go into work."

"There's a coyote invasion going on."

"Goddamn." Doug sipped his beer. "I finally kicked it in the face and he ran off, but I swear to shit he chased me for at least a mile."

"Where'd he come from?"

Doug looked across the table at me, eyes wide as planets. "He came from between our houses, Doctor. I was pulling my bike out of the garage and I looked over and he was sitting there looking at me, like he'd been waiting. He was right by your garbage cans."

"Recycling day," I said.

"At first I just thought he was one of those little dogs that look like Lassie, you know, but skinnier."

"I don't know what they're called."

"But then it showed me its teeth so I jumped on the bike and hauled ass and it started after me."

"Maybe it thought you were playing."

"I have a pistol on me, Doctor."

"Think you'll get one?"

"I don't want to, but I will if I have to. I don't want those little rats sneaking around back here with my kids playing in the sandbox." I wished I had a son like Doug, a guy with a solid job who thinks about protecting his kids until he's crazy.

"I hear that."

"Don't tell Nancy I have the gun, though. I got it a few years ago after all those abduction stories."

"I remember when I emailed those."

"That's why I got the gun. Sean was still in diapers."

Sean is his five-year-old, a blonde kid who still baby-talks, not saying his *r*s correctly. Once, when he walked up out of my basement after he'd been playing with Carl Jr. and Kenny, he said to me, "Hewo, Wes."

"Hewo, wew," I said playfully, obviously meaning, "Hello, you."

"What?" he said back.

"We should set traps," Doug said, staring into the darkness. "You want a beer?"

"I'm good," I said. "I still wonder, though, you said the dog didn't do anything until you took off. Maybe he thought you were playing."

Doug frowned. The inner edges of his eyebrows closed together. It's the look my clients give me when I tell them their benefits expired. When their eyebrows touch, that's when things start going to hell.

"Wait here," said Doug. The patio door slid open and he walked inside. When he came back out, he said, "Bait," and set down a contraption that looked like a heavy duty flashlight with a handle on top, but instead of a glass pane with a light behind it, there was a speaker. "It's called Predation," he said. "I got it at Cabela's."

"When did you get down there?"

"I took off work today and drove down. It's a game call." He pulled an antenna from the unit and walked into the darkness down to the edge of the lawn. He set it by a bush, walked back to the patio, pulled out a remote control and pressed a button. We heard a noise and my ears tingled the way my leg tingles when it falls asleep.

"Coyote howl," he said.

"That's more a yip."

He pressed the button again and said, "What's cool is this is also an MP3 player. You can go to their website and download like thirty different animal sounds."

"But you just need the coyote."

"Yeah, but if I need more, I can get more. It's just I can do more with it than just call in coyotes, if I want to. It's also got a CD with about three hundred more animal sounds." I thought of those Sounds of Nature CDs I used to listen to before I got on sleeping pills. I played them at night: waterfalls, waves, loons, all the sounds right in the speakers.

Doug pressed a button and a wolf pup whimpered from where the coyote just was. "Listen," he said, reading the user's manual. "I can play cottontail distress, fawn distress, canine pup distress, crow distress. It's got just about every kind of animal in distress."

"*Every* kind?" I said, forcing a laugh.

"Just a-goddamn-bout."

"Hey buddy," I said. "This thing's actually going to call the coyotes *in*. You sure that's what you want?"

He nodded. "I got steaks," he whispered. "The guy at Cabela's said to dip them in mouse poison and set them down by the trees. When the coyotes come in at night, they'll eat the steaks and go off and die."

"Rot away like dead mice in walls."

"What?"

"They dry up, right?" I said. "That poison shit dehydrates them."

"The guy said there's this chemical called brodifuckem or some shit in there."

"Yeah, it dehydrates them."

"I don't care if it dehydrates them," Doug said, "so long as it kills them."

"Who's going to stay up all night and call in the coyotes?" My face was hot. "Does that caller have a timer or something?"

"All I know is what the Cabela's guy told me." He stood, grabbed his beer and remote, and walked into the darkness.

Later, when the lights in Doug's house had gone off, I put on some gloves, tiptoed into his yard with a little pen-flashlight and found the steaks. I put them in a plastic Target bag and tied the top closed. On my way to work the next morning, I tossed the polluted steaks into a dumpster behind the Goodwill, rolled up the window and yipped to myself. Each day over the next couple months, I'd get a little louder until I was full-on howling, I shit you not.

Janet gets home from her Walgreens shift at ten o'clock and goes straight to the basement. Verona is scrapbooking in the bedroom and Carl and the kids are in the basement. The sweetness of what my clients call *doobage*, *skoofus* and *root* float up through the vents, and even though I'm not Catholic, I cross myself, touching forehead, belly button, left nipple, and then right.

I go to my office, lock the door and launch back into the study of the coyote to discover why it manifests in me. I sit at my cluttered desk and tear through books and Internet sites. The phone rings. Stephan.

"Wes, you gotta come back in tomorrow. I can't handle your calls."

"I have fleas," I say. Stephan doesn't know the depths of this thing, but I give him just enough to make him think my situation critical. I pinch the cordless phone between my neck and shoulder and walk to the bookshelf and free a hefty green *World Book Encyclopedia*, Volume A-C.

"You're going to lose your retirement, Wes."

"I'm a Trickster," I say. "I'm a tricky old shit."

I carry the encyclopedia across the room, kicking through books and papers splayed out across the carpet, and switch on my mini-Lexmark copier hooked to my laptop.

"I'm not trying to ride you, Wes, but I need you. Get over this dog shit, Wes."

"What dog shit, Stephan?"

"Jesus, Wes. How am I going to handle things?"

"You're being selfish," I say and spread the book across the glass surface. I press the button. The machine's gears crunch. The phone tumbles off my shoulder. I pick it up.

"You okay, Wes?"

"I have a mission. I'm working on a mission statement."

The copier spits out a tongue of paper. I snatch it and pin it into the wall-collage of miscellaneous wildlife drawings and photos. Social Services will find my room and find me "unsound." Years of experience has taught me how to provide the best evidence to support diagnosis of "instability severe enough to cause harm in the subject, either in the form of self-abuse or the probability of a severely negative effect on others."

"Wes, we're getting concerned."

"Coyotes," I say. "You can't see them but they're there. They're looking at you."

"You want to talk to Pat, Wes? I don't know what to say anymore."

"I already talked to Pat."

"I could have a mental health investigator on you in a flash, Wes."

"Ready when you are." I hang up.

Stephan will die at his desk, probably of a stroke, brain bleeding into itself, out his nose, and onto the various forms we've used for years and that are updated regularly due to ongoing policy revisions based on new legislation and presented to us through regular inter-office memos and meetings.

I stay in my office all night and lie on the couch and read. I check my email and get another one from Carl. "Dad me and Janet talked about it more and were just going ta cool out and take are time on this thing so know sweat about what I said earler peace out."

I have an awful itching underneath my chin.

I read Frank J. Dobie's *The Voice of the Coyote* and Paul Radin's *Trickster*, both of which praise the coyote as a figure of stature in Native American cultures. Radin says, "By being the buffoon, the Trickster, the satirist of the prairie, the coyote was often the savior of the people. Coyote played tricks on the unsuspecting people in hopes of saving them from themselves, to recognize their own fallen state."

Exactly what I need: documentation. Imagine the news story that would get forwarded by some other schmuck: "Old Man Thinks He's a Dog, Can't Remember Self or Family," and it's authentic because I have real dreams and physical symptoms: itching, shedding, breathing through my mouth. I'm just using them to my advantage. I'll be sentenced to St. Peter's Hospital for unbroken rest and shelter. I once read of a farmer in South Dakota who faked amnesia after he jumped off his barn while holding a live turkey over his head. He had twelve kids and a wife and banks wanting him to pony up for tractor loans, but he let the ruse slip and had to go home and auction stuff, so he cudgeled himself with a wood ax.

He didn't have his story straight, but I do.

Verona knocks on the door. "It's bedtime, Doctor. Come down here and help me get the kids out of the kitchen. They're spilling shit all over the place."

"Where's Carl?"

"He's on the computer in the middle of a goddamn game."

"I saw Janet come home."

"She's sleeping."

"Where the hell's Jennifer?"

"Good question."

Jennifer had left for her friend Kaylee's and hadn't come home. I open the door and see Verona's big eyes. Jennifer is always the first kid home.

"I'll make a call," Vonnie says. "You get Carl off his ass. I'm sick of doing his shit for him."

A new dream about the coyote had been repeating itself and expanding: this time, after eating, I froze in a field, squatted, front paws between rear, grunting. I couldn't shit. My gut felt like a bank vault.

I should be out chasing down Jennifer, but Vonnie's got it covered, so I email Carl. "Get up here, and bring some of that *skoofus* you're always burning."

The office door swings open and there's Carl in underwear and his Linkin Park t-Shirt, a bong tucked under one arm, stomach overhanging his briefs. "What's up, man?" he says.

I put my fingers to my lips. He sits down on my couch and without a word, starts packing the bong. "This is pretty trippy," he says. "Kind of awkward."

"Who owns this house?"

"You do," he says. "Is that what this is about?"

I sit at my office chair and take a hit that sends snot from my nose, and when done coughing, I tell the boy about the dream.

"It came clear, okay?" I say. "I don't need you repeating any of this, Carl."

"Are you crackin', man?" Carl's eyes are as serious and clear as they've ever been.

"Listen," I say. The back of my wrist itches so I scratch it with my top two teeth. "There's something I have to say. First, you've got your mother out looking for your daughter, like she needs that kind of crap at her age."

"She's fine," Carl says. "You gotta let kids explore, man."

"And second," I say, "This biologist for the U.S. Department of Agriculture called the coyote 'the archpredator of our times, deserving of no place of quarter.' Listen, way before the white people banged into the continent, the coyote was shaping North American values."

Carl is in the midst of an inhale, bong water bubbling.

"The coyote knows its place in the world and that's why people in power fear it."

Carl sets the bong on the coffee table and leans

forward. "You're talking my language, man. I'm pretty anti-establishment as hell."

"Quit kidding yourself, Carl. You feed off the establishment. The coyote lives on the edges, he doesn't *need* us, and that's what scares us, so we defame it. That's what the *Road Runner* cartoons were going after." I'm sweating.

"The kids watch the hell out of that one," Carl says, handing the bong toward me.

I wave him off and continue: "Listen, Wile E. Coyote is the fringe-dweller, the bird is the establishment. You see what I'm getting at?"

"Right the fuck on, I get it." Carl chokes. "You're lecturing me about responsibility with parables and shit." He holds his lighter between his second and third finger of his right hand, flipping me off with it.

I cross myself and say, "Never mind. Go back to your dog dish."

"I thought we were having some kind of father-son moment."

"Not likely." I can't get wind into my lungs. "I had a point to make, but you're the wrong guy to make it to."

"Whatever. I don't know what you're talking about, but it's bullshit and I don't have to listen to bullshit, man."

"Back to your hole," I say. "We'll have your dish out for you in the morning." Carl walks toward the door with some purpose, drops his bong and picks it back up.

I lay on the couch shivering and sweating. When my heart feels like it's going to crack through my ribs, I fling open the door. The hall is dark. I walk through the kitchen and open the patio door. Jennifer sits alone at the table outside. I reach out and run my hand through her hair.

I want to tell her what I wanted to tell her dad, that the Road Runner was a modern American lie like The Lone Ranger and GI Joe. But coyotes aren't marketable. They live their own lives, and as for their place in our society, they don't want one. And Carl was no coyote. Jennifer's dad was more like Snoopy.

In my flannel pajamas, I stand bare-footed on the cool patio and stare into the dark backyard and then up at the sky full of stars. No Northern Lights, no moon, no visible satellites. Nothing moves in the universe and I no longer feel like yelping because of Jennifer's hair touching my fingertips. She says, "We better go in."

I cross myself and say something about the Father, Son, and Holy Ghost, and know that after a short vacation, I'll look forward to my retirement party. Stephan and the other office guys will rent a banquet room at Denny's and present me with a coffee cup that has a bad golf joke on it like "Hookers do it better" or "I play golf like an outboard motor...It takes a while to get started and then putt... putt... putt." Stephan will stand up sweating and toast me as being a good guy. The ladies will put one of those black cardboard gravestones with "R.I.P." on my cubicle chair and I'll laugh as if I'm the first ever to be presented the gag. And I'll use my retirement gift, a membership to the local golf course, to spend every morning until oblivion searching the woods for my balls.

"I just needed some quiet," Jennifer says, and my face

tightens up so hard it hurts. A seven-year-old tells me she needs some quiet. I imagine her vision, of a smelly old man standing over her with rheumy eyes. Two years from retirement, a house full of bodies that need food, and her crazy grandpa trots across the lawn and disappears into the darkness. I wonder what story she'll tell when she goes back inside.

Regular Guy

Gordy's not prejudiced, but when the black family wanted to move in next door, he had to call a spade a spade, so to speak. First off, Gordy's not the kind of guy who goes around fucking with other people's properties, and second, he has data that proves colored people knock down home values, especially in cul de sacs. He got the information from work, where he's an Assistant Marketing Director for a mortgage company. Gordy is a real planner, a sensible guy. He spends most of his time in conference rooms with whiteboards and fluorescent lights and he says things like, "You got that right," and "Spot-on, Bob." Just this past week Gordy said, "I think we're on the right track here, but you never really know until the numbers come in." That sounded pretty goddamned good and got everyone nodding.

Things like that send the message that Gordy Palmer is a common-sense guy. He's been taught by Desmond Shanley's *Seven Habits of Effectiveness*—he took the seminar and bought the CD, on the company's dime— that "One must SEE effective in order BE effective."

His boss, Affirmative Mortgage, paid for him and all the other managers to go to a motivational speech marathon at the local basketball arena and he bought all kinds of shit to put up on his shelves in his office, right next to his most important item, an 8x10 photo of him and the golfer Tiger Woods at a charity golf tournament from a few years back. Affirmative Mortgage was one of the sponsors, so Gordy got his picture taken with Tiger, who Gordy thought a very articulate and sensible black guy. He got his picture taken with a lot of hockey players, too, all of whom were white.

Gordy's also the kind of guy that knows that if you want results, you have to take action. He's not one of those people who believes problems work themselves through if you just wait them out, and he's not one of those people who thinks that when you get threatened by a black guy you should sit back and take it because they have some kind of right to be pissed off at you for being a white guy. Instead, Gordy takes care of business. Gordy Palmer is a problem-solver.

When Gordy pulled into his driveway after work, he saw a real estate agent's Chevy Tahoe parked in his neighbor Doug's driveway. Doug and Nancy, both in their late thirties, had put their house up for sale. Doug took a job in Arizona for Nancy's health because she had some kind of terminal cancer and wanted to ride it out in the sunlight and dry heat.

A silver Cadillac Deville was parked behind the agent's SUV. Gordy guessed it was about a 2000 model, probably got it used. Four people climbed out, two adults and two kids. Gordy figured the man was the father or boyfriend, the woman the mother or girlfriend, and the two kids belonged to one of them, or both, or there were from a mix of parents, not to sound prejudiced. Their faces, what Gordy could see of them, were hard and leathery like gorillas, but that's not racist. The people Gordy worked with, the people on the committees, had hard faces, too, and none of them were black. Time and bullshit did that to people, white, black, Hmong. Whatever. Time made everyone look like gorillas.

When Gordy pulled into his driveway, he looked at the blacks first and then at his own son, Chuck, who was working on his 1978 Impala that Gordy bought him on the condition that he go into drug rehab and also quit cigarettes. He wore a grease-smeared sleeveless white t-shirt. His stringy arms leaned into the radiator, a cigarette pinched in his lips as he stared down at the engine block. He wore one of those New York Yankees baseball caps with the pancake-flat bill hanging sideways off his shaved head. He acted like a black kid and talked like one, too, Gordy thought, just to piss off his old man, not that Gordy cared one way or the other.

Gordy climbed out of his rig, stood still and stared until Chuck noticed him. Chuck took a drag from his smoke and said, "Whatchoo lookin' at?" and blew smoke toward Gordy.

"Hey, guy," said Gordy. "I don't want to lecture you about the cancer sticks, but we had an agreement here."

"Whatchoo think," Chuck said, "I can quit the booze

and smokes alls at once? Watchoo think, I'm Supa-man?"

Gordy mumbled "Supa-man" and walked inside. If it weren't for the blacks and the real estate agent in Doug's driveway staring over at them, Gordy would have yelled something back.

Gordy had a good view of Doug's house from the breakfast nook that he'd added onto the side of the house four years ago when his wife died. He used part of the life insurance money to make some changes and move forward, so to speak. Since the breakfast nook windows were tinted somewhat, he thought he could look out and no one could see in. He watched the two black kids. They wore gray hooded sweatshirts even though it was eighty degrees outside and had their hands in their pockets, looking down at the driveway. The woman looked down, too, and no one talked to the agent except for the man. The wife and kids didn't raise their eyes, even when they walked toward the house, the real estate agent leading the way and rotating like a dancer, swinging her arms out to present them the neighborhood. The man wore jeans and a black sweatshirt, which reminded Gordy of *The Cosby Show*, how Cliff Huxtable always wore college sweatshirts. Gordy couldn't tell if the man's sweatshirt had a college logo, so he went for his binoculars in the kitchen junk drawer.

The front door slammed and he tucked the binoculars behind him into the cabinet where he kept the phone books.

Chuck walked in, sweating and breathing hard. "We

got munch?" he said. He threw his keys on the table in front of Gordy, opened the refrigerator door, snagged a bottle of water, held it straight up and guzzled, bubbles rising up through the bottle like an office water cooler.

"Close the door," Gordy said. "You're air-conditioning the neighborhood."

Chuck put his forefinger in the air, the "hang on a minute" sign, drained the bottle, threw it into the sink and walked upstairs, his underwear puffing out from his jeans like a deflated chef's hat.

Gordy closed the refrigerator door and looked out into Doug's backyard. He saw the blonde real estate agent float across the back patio, and the blacks followed behind like ducks. Then the father spun around, dropped to one knee and clutched one of the boy's arms. At first he shook the kid, and then held him still, talking into his face. Then he suddenly looked in Gordy's direction like a deer that heard a twig snap. He released the boy and stood, squinting at the breakfast nook and holding his hand over his brow ridge like a salute to get a better look. Gordy backed up into the corner of the countertop and poked his kidney. He clenched his teeth and said "Fuck."

He rubbed his kidney, poured a scotch and went into his office to Google a solution. He was a little nervous typing in "house" along with "sabotage" because the government might flag him and guys in suits would show up at the door and look into his eyes for answers, but then he remembered that when he was a kid and his parents put their house up for sale, right before a showing, he spread mud around the bathtub and sink and then he took a big shit and didn't flush it, and his old man spanked his ass until his tailbone bruised. The people didn't buy the house, though.

But who would punish Gordy fifty years later if he sneaked into the next door neighbor's house and spread dirt around the patio, maybe spray-painted some stuff on the windows or took a leak at the base of the patio door so that when the sun erupted the next day, the piss fermented into the smell of portable toilets at a county fair? Who'd make him ashamed? His wife, Gordy's moral guide, got killed off by a lung tumor four years earlier, and his kid didn't give a shit about shit. Gordy could kill a guy and Chuck would say, "We got chow?"

Chuck was a laid-back kid. Once, when Chuck was twelve, Gordy found the boy power-washing his Chevy Tahoe, which was brand new. Gordy woke up around noon on a Saturday, chugged three glasses of water to fight off the scotch hangover, squinted his way out the front door onto the hot sidewalk in his bare feet, and smelled the hot steam burning off the driveway. When he turned the corner, a spray covered him, and it felt good until he saw the chipped paint on the driver's side door. Chuck was just starting to wear his ball cap backwards. "Wassup, Dad?" he said, turning off the spray.

"Come in for a second," Gordy said, and when Chuck walked in the door, Gordy smacked him on the side of the head with an open hand. Chuck dropped to the floor and did a push-up to spring himself back up. Gordy's wife, who was in a wheelchair in the kitchen with oxygen tubes sticking up her nose, started breathing heavier.

Chuck said, "It's cool, Ma," as he walked past her and patted her bony shoulder through her robe. "I don't let shit get to me. That's just how I roll."

So anyway, if Gordy got caught pissing on a neighbor's patio, there'd be some public shame, but if he admitted to a drinking problem, he could go to rehab—insurance would pay and he had plenty of sick leave—and he'd also get an "attaboy" from his supervisor, who has a poster of the "Twelve Steps to Recovery" in fancy lettering on the wall behind his desk.

Out of the twenty members of the company's Leadership Team, on which Gordy represented the marketing division, there was one cripple, one lesbian, one black, and the rest were regular white heterosexuals. The cripple, Allan, was paraplegic and always said "dialogue" as a verb, as in, "I think the most valuable aspect of this group is that we all like to dialogue about these issues." Sometimes, he joked about his condition. Once, he and Gordy were eating lunch at the conference table, buffet-style sandwiches and diet pop, and Gordy said, "I just got some gel insoles for my achy heels. They're a real godsend."

"Insoles won't do me much good," Allan said.

Gordy respected that joke because Allan couldn't feel his feet *at all*. Allan had a disadvantage in life, but he still achieved a professional career, established respect, and most of all, had a sense of humor about his disorder. Sam Washington was the opposite. He was one of those black guys who'd had hard luck and overcompensated for it by being a know-it-all.

Sam Washington was one of the first black guys Gordy'd ever hired, and no one can call Gordy prejudiced because he'd hired more than one. Gordy usually associated the name "Sam" with bow ties and sweater vests rather than hooded sweatshirts, which is funny because Sam wore bow ties and sweater vests. Sam was what's called an "Oreo Cookie," which meant he was dark on the outside, white on the inside, like Bryant Gumbel and Colin Powell.

Once, Gordy took Sam to the zoo and showed him his favorite display, the cougar pen. It was something Gordy did for all the new employees he brought on board, to build trust and help them "get to know Gordy," so to speak, to inform them that he was a regular guy but also hard-assed if he had to be, if you forced his hand, and that's why he showed them the cougar, of which he also had a portrait in his office, along with a framed adoption certificate. "Curt the Cougar" was Gordy Palmer's officially adopted pet for one hundred fifty bucks a year. It showed that Gordy cared about the broader world. Gordy was a big-picture kind of guy.

Gordy and Sam sipped roast coffee from the Starbucks booth, Gordy's treat, both of them wearing beige trench coats because they were partially outside in a semi-covered heated plexiglass tube smeared with kid snot and hand oil that led through the woodsy exhibits that recreated the northern habitats of mink, cougars, wolverine, red foxes, otters, beavers, gray wolves, eagles, and Curt, Gordy's cougar. The "Creatures of the North Woods" exhibit.

They watched Curt pace his usual pattern, skulking down into a plaster canyon then up a cliff to a three-foot wide plateau where he paused and looked out through the thin black wire mesh that covered the upper reaches of the display, and then he stalked back down the canyon and back up again, repeating the pattern.

"Reminds me," Sam said, out of nowhere, without Gordy starting the conversation, "of that polar bear at the St. Paul Zoo. You ever see him?" He didn't pause for Gordy to answer. "Its water tank is fifteen feet deep and twenty feet long, and for hours the bear just slinks off the edge of the tank, nosedives for the opposite end, curls around and shoves back, climbs to the edge, slinks back down off the edge, nosedives for the other end, and on and on." Sam shook his head. "It's really sad," he said. "It's obvious psychological damage."

Gordy explained to Sam that it was ridiculous to think that animals could have psychological problems since they couldn't "reason" like humans. "Animals can't think," Gordy said. "I think you're way off base there."

"Listen," Sam said. "It's the same effect cages have on humans." Gordy's heartbeat picked up; the guy actually told him, "Listen." Sam kept lecturing: "There was a documentary back in the late sixties. This filmmaker brought a camera into a mental institution in Connecticut. Through this opening in the door, he filmed the interior of a room with no windows, just walls, cement floor, a floor drain, and a naked old man who used to teach college English, sneering and grunting at the camera and stomping around the cell, raising his thighs and pounding his feet on the floor. He moved in a circle and stomped in rhythm, like a primitive response to confinement, just like the bear. Going crazy is just something that animals do."

Gordy worked up a smile and said, "Okay, Sam. We agree to disagree on that one."

"Stan."

"What?"

"My name is *Stan*, not *Sam*."

Gordy didn't argue. Some of them, he'd learned, thought they knew everything. Once they got some success and learned how to speak, they needed to broadcast it to the world, and Gordy understood that, so he backed off.

After Chuck cranked up his car and drove to Denny's, where he bussed tables and washed dishes, Gordy ate a box of microwaveable beef stroganoff and then filled a glass with scotch and ice and walked over to Ray's house, which was just on the other side of Doug's house in the cul de sac. Ray was the cul de sac's State Patrol officer— every cul de sac had a cop—and every Friday night, some neighbors gathered in his driveway to sit around the fire, which burned in a black metal tub on wheels with an encircling screen and a metal lid on top. Gordy brought his own lawn chair, the kind you fold into a bag and carry over your shoulder. Tonight was just Ray and his wife Deena at the fire. Gordy was early and on his fourth scotch.

Deena said, "Hey Gordy, we were just talking about that little kid who got alcohol poisoned. Did you hear about that?"

Ray sat next to her and rubbed his crew-cut. "It was in North Minneapolis," he said. "I had a buddy on that call."

"The news said the parents were in the kitchen playing poker, Deena said, "and the kids were in the basement drinking."

"The big kids let the little kids drink whiskey," said Ray. "A real sad deal."

"I don't know how they can live like that," Gordy said. And then a hand clamped his shoulder. He turned and saw his neighbor Doug unfolding his own lawn chair.

"And how are we tonight?" Doug asked in his monotone voice. He had a gentle bearing and always talked like he was educated, even though he worked in a cubicle in a building next to Home Depot. He worked for a company that developed websites for other companies.

Gordy was getting warmed from scotch, so he figured he'd just go ahead and ask: "So, let's cut to the chase here, Doug. You got any offers on your house yet?"

"We're talking to some people." Doug sipped beer. "It's about time. We had to lower the price twice already."

"Buyer's market," said Ray. "No shit about that, right Gordy?"

"You don't want to lower the price too much, though," Gordy said. "You gotta be careful about how that drives down property values across the black."

"You mean 'the block'?" Doug said.

"The board," Gordy said. "Across the board."

"We get the drift," said Ray, reaching out and slapping Gordy's knee like he was joking. The corners of Ray's lips curled up, but not too much, and then he frowned when he saw Deena's eyebrows move closer together. The fire crackled through the silence.

"I'm just shitting about things," said Gordy, "but there is a minority factor deal here. I have research to prove it. If you're interested."

"What minority deal?" said Doug. "What are you talking about?"

Doug and Ray and Deena drank and looked into the fire. Gordy plowed on. "Listen, I've been around real estate for a long time in a professional capacity," he said. "And I'm from the marketing end of the spectrum, so I know how markets work. I do the research. I know the numbers. This is just factual economic information. It'd be irresponsible of me not to bring it up, so there you go." He put his drink between his thighs, rubbed his hands together like he was washing them and then held them toward the fire to dry. "That's all she wrote. Say no more. No need to shoot the messenger here."

"These are some nice people," said Doug, his voice rising a little bit. "I think you're being unfair."

"All I'm saying is there's data. I'm just the messenger here. I'm just thinking about the neighborhood, the big picture and all that."

Ray's knees bounced and the ice in his glass tinkled, Deena coughed, and Doug drank from his Budweiser.

"Anyway, Doug," said Deena. "Did you hear about that poor little girl in Minneapolis?"

"Terrible," said Doug. He shook his head.

"So," Gordy said, staring at Doug, "you pretty close to a deal?"

"We have another showing tomorrow," said Doug, looking from Deena to the fire and then to Gordy. He made split-second eye-contact with everyone, eyes sweeping like searchlights. "Hell, I better get in and check on Nancy."

Doug stood and Gordy sort of fell toward him, mouth open, but instead of saying something smart, he straightened up and looked into the fire and said, "Have a good one there, Doug."

Here's what Gordy saw, no shit about it: every time the black family came for a showing, all three times, the man of the family would look over into Gordy's backyard like he was casing the house, and he always wore a squinty frown like one of those old-timer gorillas at the zoo, the old-man one that sat on its haunches and leered at the audience with drippy lips and puffy eyebrows. No shit about it, Gordy knew what Gordy knew. There was no getting around it. Might as well stare it in the face.

After Ray and Deena's fire, and when Chuck was at work, Gordy pulled down the shades in the breakfast nook, poured scotch and watched a movie on the TV he'd mounted on a shelf up in the corner. It was another movie about a guy hiding Jews from Nazis. He shook his head and kept his glass full, and a little after midnight when he was drunk, Gordy put on his cul de sac camouflage: navy blue work slacks, black socks and loafers with bows on them, and latex medical gloves he wore when throwing salt on his driveway. He slipped on a black windbreaker and a black Gatsby hat he wore to work in winter to look like he was thinking about how he looked. As he turned off the lights and walked to the sliding glass door that led to the back patio, his chest felt full, like a Scottish warrior readying to attack a neighboring clan.

He opened the sliding door and stepped out. The only house visible from Doug's backyard besides his own was Wes's on the other side. Wes's back corner kitchen window faced Doug's backyard. All the lights were off in both Wes's and Doug's houses, so Gordy tiptoed across Doug's lawn, hands out in front of him like a blind man feeling the air for bumps.

Gordy stepped onto Doug's patio. It was starting to rain, so he moved fast. He nudged up to the patio door, leaned his forehead on the glass and unzipped. His penis had shrunk to a nervous knot. He couldn't piss and his bladder was ready to tear. He thought of his prostate and remembered the time his doctor had said, "We're little on the large end up here but no need for alarm" when he had extracted his gloved finger from Gordy's anus with a sucking noise.

Gordy groaned, the steam from his mouth moistening the glass door, and then steam rose from below, a trickle from his dick and then an eruption. The stream smacked the glass like a power washer and sprayed back, so Gordy turned left, and when he swung around he saw a light in Wes's kitchen window and a dark spot moving and then the light snapped off and Gordy zipped up fast and cupped his package, piss dribbling through his fingers.

Then he was inside Doug's house. He didn't remember opening the sliding glass door. He figured he must have panicked, trying to hide from Wes's window, and went inside. He also realized that he crapped his pants a little bit, from booze or nerves, or both, and then he looked down and saw Doug's novelty entry-rug with the white script letters that always made him laugh, except for this time. It said:

Welcome.

Now, wipe your goddamn feet!

Gordy slid open the door and closed it behind him, gently, and he didn't hear the rain anymore once he got outside. He stood and swayed on Doug's patio and smiled a little, even though he'd pissed and shit himself. A guy has to do what a guy has to do. Then he aimed for his yard, and once there, he lay down in the grass to take a break. He'd never seen the world from the lawn's point of view. He looked up for the stars, except there were none, and he covered his left eye with his hand just to make sure. The sky was a low gray sheet of clouds, visible only by struggling street lights, and it all started to rotate. Then he shut his eyes, but started to spin more, this time from the inside. He rolled to his side and puked in the grass.

Chuck stumbled through the front door at three in the morning, stumbling not because he was drunk, but tired. He'd worked the Denny's kitchen-pit from five in the evening to one in the morning, and afterwards, he helped with some kitchen clean-up and drank coffee with a new server named Alexis, who had a diamond in her left nostril and two kids. It was either that or go home and listen to the old man mumbling behind his office door.

So Chuck sat and listened to Alexis's life story. Alexis was twenty-one and liked her new job because she liked talking to people, and Chuck liked listening to her. She'd lost her mom to cancer, too, and her dad was an asshole.

"My old man's an asshole, too," Chuck told her. "But he's a pretty good guy under all the shit. He's just been dealin' with a lot of shit."

When Chuck got home, he walked upstairs, peeled off his food-smeared uniform, balled it up and threw it in his clothes hamper. He stuck his head out the window to have a smoke before hitting the sack and saw Gordy laying on his back on the back lawn, looking like a homicide victim. He'd never seen Gordy passed out outside in the yard like this, and he finished his smoke before walking down to help him.

When he knelt to grab his dad's armpits, he smelled the shit and piss and puke. He rolled Gordy over onto his stomach and saw the smeared pants, so he pulled off the old man's loafers and yanked off his slacks, pulling by the cuffs, and then he went to the garage and wheeled out the power washer. He plugged in the compressor, which rumbled loudly, set the spray beam on wide and blasted the shit out of Gordy's trousers until they rolled up against the house in a clump. Gordy tried to climb to his knees and grapple the gun away from Chuck, but Chuck just moved backwards and Gordy fell onto his stomach, exposing his stained underwear. That's when Chuck narrowed the spray beam and started cleaning his father in a more systematic manner. Chuck heard something like a weak sobbing as mist filled the air.

Doug's back light came on and he walked across the lawn in a robe as Chuck was spraying his father's ass and legs. Gordy leaned on his arms, staring forward, and Chuck then rolled him onto his back and moved the beam of spray up his belly to avoid hitting his genitals, the water beads like BBs, and the jet force pushed Gordy's shirt and jacket up over his face. As Gordy tried to stand, he struggled with his jacket-covered head, Chuck let go of the trigger and with Gordy leaning forward, pulled off his soaked jacket and shirt and threw them on the lawn. Gordy staggered around in only his underwear and squinted at Doug and Chuck.

"Jesus," said Doug. "This is different."

The air compressor shut off since the gun was turned off.

"What the goddamn," Gordy stammered, putting his hands on his bare hips. "What the goddamn."

"I'm washin' the shit off you," Chuck said.

"Watch your mouth." Gordy squinted, trying to look mad.

"Let's get him inside," said Doug.

"I'm fine," Gordy said. "I'm just doing a thing here. For everyone's thing."

"You pissed in my house, Gordy."

"And you shit yourself," Chuck said.

"I know that." Gordy moved toward Doug, tugging up the elastic on his underwear. "But a guy can't wait around for things. A guy's gotta do it himself."

"Nice touch with the power washer," Doug said to Chuck. "I never seen one used that way before."

"Na-funny," said Gordy, trying hard to stand still. He puffed out his chest, and then he said, almost formally, "This is not funny." Then he turned and stumbled toward the patio door.

"Can't be bringin' this kinda shit out in the open," Chuck said, and then he walked to the patio door to open it for Gordy, who was leaning his face down to the handle to get a good look. When he slid open the door, Gordy felt his way inside, and before Chuck closed the door, he looked back at Doug and said, "Serious shit, dawg."

"Serious," said Doug, and then he walked back across the lawn. Both patio lights winked out at the same time, and the power washer, still plugged in, woke up and started grumbling into the darkness.

Part Two

The Ballad
of Gary Wiegard

Where the Kids Go

Gary and Liz strip off the kids' winter coats and stuff them into the cargo net beneath Peter's Power Stroller, the most advanced stroller on the market. It was a present from Gary's employees at the truss company for the new baby still inside Liz, but Peter had already claimed it. Peter, who is four, sleeps in the stroller while six-year-old Heather is slung over Peter's left shoulder like a halibut. The stroller has an electrically retractable sun visor, rain visor, and built-in cup holders. Gary wonders why he has kids.

The family queues up for tickets along a plexiglass wall that overlooks an auditorium. Down below is the 1998 St. Paul Winter Carnival Fun-Fest, a children's fair with games, rides, booths selling craft items, tutoring programs, guitar lessons. The Gary and Liz Wiegard quest: to help Peter see Thomas the Tank Engine live and in person, the featured event. Gary is so tired that a sheen of sweat issues from his forehead like one of those living room waterfalls that runs down glass, and he forgets to wipe it.

Liz hands Gary a bottle of Poland Spring water and opens her purse for the checkbook. Gary looks down at the auditorium floor at waves of heads moving between vendor booths, rides, inflatable play structures, food stands, and upright video games that wall the central aisle. He can't see faces, only skulls and backs and shoulders bent over the machines.

"I'm so goddamn tired," Gary tells the plexiglass. He hasn't slept for days, overseeing a big contract at his company. His company promised a cul de sac developer a custom-designed set of trusses to up the roofs of twelve houses. The Sands of Pines development. Gary has no idea what The Sands of Pines means, but he's not one to ask about marketing decisions. Instead, he does his own job, which is to provide framing support for suburban homes. He's an infrastructure guy. That's what his grandfather taught Gary before he croaked and gave Gary and his dad the company, which Gary now pretty much runs because his dad retired: do what the client says to do.

"What?" Liz turns. "What did you say? You look exhausted." Liz writes a check.

Gary turns away from the stroller and looks at the mother behind him who clutches a double-stroller with dry hands that have shed particles of dry skin onto the blue fabric of the stroller hood.

"I'm a devoted father," he says.

She stares down the hall, pretending to have heard nothing. Her two identical curly-topped toddlers in the double-stroller rotate their heads like animatronic characters. The mother wears hoop earrings like shower curtain rings and a Minnesota Vikings sweater with a white turtleneck underneath. Her face flakes underneath a coat of rouge. Gary would guess she's his same age, thirty, or maybe a bit older, but she looks way older.

Gary wonders if she has a husband to help her out with routine maintenance. He tries to catch her eyes to send an empathetic glance. Does she have weekend visitation, maybe? What, for instance, would Liz do without Gary? He did what a lot of guys didn't: changed diapers, wiped butts, applied unguent, strapped kids into car seats, actions that had become so automatic that he feared he'd misplace a kid, leave it in the back seat of the car on an August day as he walked into work, or allow the stroller to roll down a hill while he stared up at a cloud that looked like a cabbage.

"Are you a good parent?" Gary turns to ask the plexiglass, hoping the sound will reach the woman. He starts to giggle and his eyes water.

"What's wrong with you?" Liz says.

Gary thinks the woman has the eyes of a caged bear. She needs some room to walk around on all fours and roar and maybe graze a little bit. Peter sleeps in the Power Stroller, head lolled onto his right shoulder, looking dead.

Gary forgets the woman and looks down at acres of hairy skulls walking on the arena floor on quivering bodies. The heads palpitate against one another like crowded chicken babies in an incubator. Gary presses his fingertips into the glass and feels a vibrato quivering: the thrumming of collective windpipes and music and farting air compressors that fill the inflatable play rides that shake from the rising and falling of kid feet and diapered butts.

"This is massive," Gary says. "There's something wrong here."

At the ticket booth, a black woman peels tickets from a pink roll the size of a steering wheel. She calls out the dollar total through a rectangular microphone welded into the center of the window, the same kind used at liquor stores in bad neighborhoods.

"Wake up!" Gary screams down at Peter.

Liz turns. "Why are you yelling?"

"Power Rangers," Peter says, snapping awake and rubbing his forehead.

Gary lifts his pale cheeks into a grin and Liz turns away, eyebrows knotted. Heather drips saliva onto Gary's shirt. The saliva stains his right shoulder, and looks to Gary like a map of western Wisconsin with the Indian-head nose, as they call it, or a stereotypical profile of a Jewish nose.

Gary blinks to moisten his eyeballs. He isn't sure he could support another baby, but there's his wife with another swelled belly due to another baby inside it. Number three. He doesn't mean he couldn't support it economically. He's not sure what he means.

"Are we pregnant again?" he says, laughing. Liz doesn't hear. When Liz was pregnant with Peter, Gary gained twenty-seven pounds of sympathy fat. He never lost it.

"I'm freaked out," he says, grinning.

"What?"

"Let's get some cotton candy."

Maybe the reason Gary hasn't slept all week isn't just because of the cul de sac project, but because last weekend, the weekend before the Fun-Fest, he sat beside Peter at a fountain in a suburban mall and watched an infant drop into the water and die. The baby's mother sat to Gary's right, on the ledge of the fountain with her back to the water. She spoke to a woman who stood and twirled a plastic bag full of shoes around her wrist until it wrapped tight. Then she swung it back the other way, beginning a new loop every time an old one closed. The infant belly-crawled across the ledge and stretched for the water in imitation of what Peter was doing, but Peter was four and had some fine motor skills. Both kids lay on their stomachs, dangling fingers into the water while Gary watched the mother. Sensing motion, the mom twisted sideways and reached back to sling an index finger into the infant's diaper above his butt crack. As the women talked, Gary could only hear the monotone hum of shoppers' voices blend with the static of high-pressured water, fine jets shooting out laterally in thin exploding globes of mist that evaporated over shoppers' heads. Gary noticed the baby tumble into the pool, but only peripherally, because along with watching the swinging bag, he was watching the profile of the mother's right breast backlit through a white blouse.

After it fell, Gary looked down and the boy looked back up at him through rippled water littered with cellophane, plastic, and skinny bits of paper from price tags. Gary saw floating bug parts: tiny legs like freshly cut whiskers, black shells of beetles like burnt peanut slivers. Beneath bug fragments, the infant's grinning face shimmered. Circles of chocolate smeared his puffy cheeks. When the mother reached down and hauled up the body, the chocolate remained.

Liz didn't see it. She was off with Heather shopping for new baby bedding while Gary and Peter rested on the cement ledge that enclosed the circle of foot-deep water. Liz had said, when they parted, "Don't let Peter stick his hands in the water. It's cold." She said that because Peter had started antibiotics for bronchitis two weeks earlier. And as soon at Peter got better, he wanted to meet Thomas the Tank Engine. It never ended.

From the Fun-Fest ticket line, Gary and Liz walk toward the elevator with the kids, directed by a sign on a shaky silver post that reads, "Strollers Use Elevator." They fall into a long line of heel-bumping strollers clutched by parents who lean on one leg, and then the other, waiting. Gary sets down Heather, who wobbles, yawns, and looks around. He grabs the back axle of the stroller, Peter still inside, with his left hand and the front axle with his right, lifts with his knees, and hoists the stroller—stuffed with a forty-pound kid and four jackets, along with a purse, diaper bag, water bottle, wet wipes, camera, and fish cracker snacks—sideways across his chest. He creeps away from the queue of people waiting at the elevator and walks down the steps, his lower spine sidling the handrail as he nudges the stroller into the opposing bodies that walk up the stairs. Liz breathes hard behind Gary under the strain of the alien biological organism in her gut.

A gray-haired lady struggles up the steps and smiles at Peter in the stroller. Peter suddenly shudders and yells, "Peter Pan!" and it seems to Gary that the rising parents, eyes glossy and cheeks bloodless like office workers heading back to their cubicles after a smoke break, have lost their children. They walk up the stairs alone, childless. Their kids are gone.

"Where are all these people's kids?" Gary asks Liz as they reach the auditorium floor and he sets down the stroller with Peter still in it.

"I told you to stay home and sleep," says Liz, holding little Heather's hand. "I could have done this on my own."

Gary never sleeps, partly because of the kids and in part because of the way his brain works. He can have five scotches with no mixers before bed and still be sober and awake. He knows it'll catch up to him when he's older, but for now, it's all he can do to shut himself down to sleep. A couple of weeks ago, for instance, even after Gary had drunk a half a pint of scotch while celebrating Christmas Eve, he drove Peter to the emergency room at 1 a.m. because the clear snot he'd been coughing up for weeks turned deep brown and smelled like mold. It was on Christmas Eve around midnight that the fluid hardened. Peter could only breathe if he lay cheek-down on the pillow, head sideways, arms folded beneath his chest and knees curled up to his hands, ass in the air and lungs sloped down just enough so gravity could stretch open a bronchial tube.

Liz and Gary, deep into the morning, lay in their bed listening to the lung-gurgle from across the hall. "We should take him in," Liz said.

"He's just over-exhausted," Gary said. Peter had been building couch forts with his cousins all evening during the Christmas Eve get-together at Gary's brother Lyle's house. "He's just played out."

"I can't sleep with the noise."

"If we go to the doctor, we'll just get antibiotics and he's going to build up a resistance." Gary yawned. "Think about it. The wheezing we're hearing is his immune system battling bugs. It's getting stronger."

They went to the emergency room anyway. Liz insisted.

Gary sets the stroller on the auditorium floor and looks up. Thirty-foot-tall slides quiver in air-pressured heft as they spit children onto padded landing areas. The kids tumble into springy backstops, many laughing, screaming, others wiping snot from their faces with forearms as hairy ride attendants in blue t-shirts lift them down onto gym mats where their shoes lay and their parents stand, most of them with their legs crossed, arms folded, lips tights, eyebrows narrowed.

The steep and bouncy slides don't concern Gary, though, as he merges Peter and his stroller into a stream of moving bodies and glances over his shoulder for Liz, who waddles in pregnancy and tows Heather by the hand. Some of the inflatable jumpers are cartoon characters. Animals quiver on fat haunches: Scooby Doo, Garfield, and a squatting Snoopy with a Buddha belly and a gaping hole in its elevated mouth where sweating toddlers are upchucked. The kids enter Snoopy's butt, scale his alimentary canal, and escape through his mouth to descend the groove of his red tongue. The cartoon animals smile.

The rides shorten and thicken the further the family moves into the hall. These are rides for the smaller kids. Turrets of inflatable castles named "Excalibur" and "Camelot" wiggle as children bounce. A Pooh Bear, legs straddled and hand dipping into a honey pot that serves as an entryway, shakes his rumbly tumbly with the help of little kids flailing around inside. Finally, to Gary's satisfaction, the original inflatable bouncer, the "Space Invaders" of inflatable play toys appears, a red, white, and blue "Moonwalk," a simple round blow-up dome entered into by pushing aside two swinging flaps stained with hand grease.

In the old Moonwalks when he was a kid, children would jump on a pad with a bulge in the middle that moved them to the sides where they would press their faces against smeared clear plastic and make pig faces at their parents. Unlike the Moonwalks of Gary's childhood, however, this one has no windows. He can't see the kids inside. He can just see the quivering of the rubber generated by the bouncing interior bodies, and then stillness, and then more kids taking off their shoes and going inside. He doesn't see any kids coming out.

"What the fuck?" he says toward Liz. He's stopped in a stream of moving bodies that pass around him like leaves around a log in a river. "Where are the kids going?"

As Gary stops, Liz takes the lead with Heather dragging behind and pointing, mouthing aloud the things she wants. They walk by popcorn blowers, cotton candy wheels, video game islands, clicking wooden roulette wheels with yellow and black slots, where the black prizes are plastic spider rings and the yellow prizes are either conical suckers or blue stuffed animals the size of fists. They pass a U.S. Army booth where three grinning soldiers stand beside a fifteen-foot inflatable rubber soldier and guide its quivering hand the size of a first baseman's glove toward frightened children. Then they pass a booth for missing children where two lonely-looking women lean over a table stacked with fresh piles of brochures and bumper stickers.

"There," says Gary, standing on his toes and pointing to a stage that fills the north wall of the auditorium; the expectant crowd of human-led strollers extends outward one hundred yards. A giant fake roundhouse with curtains pulled across the front sits up on the stage. Children dance in front of the stage to stereo-belted kid's music with fun beats in anticipation of the grinning train engines seen only on TV that will soon poke out their iron snoots and go "Toot-toot, friends!" This is the stage that is set up for the Thomas the Tank Engine appearance that Peter wanted to see so badly.

"I don't want to go," Peter says. "I want to bounce."

"We paid fifty bucks to see Thomas," Gary says.

"We're watching the show."

"I don't want to. I'm hungry."

"It's his day." Liz squeezes Gary's forearm. "Let's trade kids. You take Heather and I'll take Peter."

Gary lifts Peter from the Power Stroller and holds him to his shoulder; he's only four but weighs as much as his six-year-old sister. Liz places Heather, still the size of a four-year-old, in the stroller and she grins, gazing up at a bundle of balloons that had become detached and wrapped around a ceiling girder.

"All this hassle for the fucking train and he doesn't give a shit now," Gary says.

"He just woke up. He's hungry."

"Get him a goddamn hot dog."

"Cotton candy," Peter screams, and then starts to cry like he's just snapped his ankle, and he squeezes Gary's ears in his tiny fists. Gary bats the boy's hands away.

"I'll get in line for a ride and you go get food," says Gary. "Or else the opposite. I don't give a shit. What should I do for the boy?"

"Give him a break," Liz says. "He just got over bronchitis."

"Yeah, well," says Gary.

Two weeks earlier, after they had gone to the emergency room and gotten the bronchitis diagnosis, Liz, Peter, and Heather stayed in the van while Gary stumbled through the Wal-Mart parking lot to the twenty-four hour pharmacy to get the "bug killer" the doctor had prescribed for Peter. Gary leaned into a wind that wrapped a yellow shopping bag across his shin.

When he got inside, a blue-coated pharmacy woman handed him a brochure on "Viral Infections" when he turned over the prescription note. It read, "Bronchitis is an inflammation of the mucous membrane that lines the main passages of the lungs. It starts by a common cold bug, one of two hundred forms, that spreads into the lungs and takes root."

Gary set the pamphlet on the counter and walked away while the prescription was being filled, pausing in front of the birth control aisle, rubbing his eyes and wondering whether contraceptive sponges were still sold. Liz used them when they were younger and fighting through college and not wanting a kid yet. They used them instead of condoms when banging, and Gary's throat would contract when after sex Liz sat on the toilet and extracted the moist globe by a string, the popping sound of air softening his knees.

A thump made his head snap to attention. He felt a tickle in his heels, followed by a child's howl. A toddler had tumbled from a shopping cart while its mother had moved off; the child had fallen straight back, shoulder blades hitting the floor and the weight of the body snapping the skull on polished tile like a beaver tail smacking a stream. Instead of rushing to the child, though, Gary turned back to the pharmacy window, hoping Peter's medicine was ready. He had to worry about his own boy.

"Thank god the kid cried," the pharmacy woman said. She'd heard the whole event. No ambulances seemed to be on the way. Gary had heard the same theory: if a kid smacks its skull and doesn't cry, the brain may be bleeding onto itself. Kids were getting damaged everywhere.

The boy who fell into the mall's water fountain a week after the Wal-Mart kid dropped never cried. Instead, he smiled, and his clear white eyes, unaffected by chlorine, fixed on Gary. Gary saw luminous eyes, circles of chocolate, Dairy Queen or Fanny Farmer's, smearing his cheeks.

The mother with the side-lit breasts laid her infant son on the floor and jabbed her fingers into his chest as though copying fragments of instruction collaged from TV shows on infant CPR, but she seemed to press too hard on the delicate chest. Gary stepped forward to help but a mall security guard arrived and dipped to his knees, nudging away the mother. She knelt and looked up at Gary with huge eyes. He almost reached for her, but she yelped and covered her mouth, face contorting as if Gary were the most frightening thing.

When Gary turned toward Peter, the boy was reaching into the water for what looked like a black beetle or a piece of candy, a Goober or a distorted malted-milk ball. "Its legs are moving," Peter said.

Gary picked him up and held him so he faced backwards over his shoulder rather than toward the "resuscitation event," which is what a voice from a walkie-talkie at the hip of an arriving emergency technician named it. Two EMTs arrived, and one, a blond man with a wide chest, set the limp infant over his thigh. He slapped the back with a cupped hand as though trying to elicit a burp, but water in the lungs wasn't the matter. What mattered was the expanding lump on the top of his skull, at the fontanelle, the thin membrane protecting the infant brain.

When the EMT recognized the purple swelling, he stood and pressed the boy gently against his shoulder and secured the back of his neck with a wide palm. He aimed for the exit as the other EMT fitted an oxygen mask over the boy's chocolate-smeared face and followed.

"What happened?" Peter said, squirming.

"The little boy got sick on chocolate."

"What kind?"

As Gary queues up with Peter for a ride on the most sophisticated inflatable at the Fun-Fest, the Mega Obstacle Challenge, he yawns so hard that a knot forms on the tendons on the underside of his chin; he rubs it until it turns from a golf ball into a malted milk ball and then disappears. Kids at the front of the long, serpentine line toss their shoes in a high pile on a gym mat. From fifty yards, the shoe stack looks to Gary like a pile of books ready to be ignited on a Polish street during World War Two. He'd just seen a World at War program about how the Nazis burned Jewish people's books in public streets. Gary shakes his head and laughs, trying to slough off the weird connection.

The kids enter the elevated obstacle by being lifted and tossed up by a teenage carnival attendant, climb a blue hill at a forty-five degree angle, plunge down a slide, scale a wall that leads to another slide that plummets them into a zone of tackle dummies on bungee cords, and once they bounce through with beaten cheeks and mussed hair, they swing by rope over a fake water-pit and then scale a bloated red tongue that leads into a giant clown face. Mountain climbing screw-holds speckle the tongue like canker sores.

"Where do the kids go?" a mother asks the ride-attendant teenager who lifts her boy onto the launching pad. The boy rolls, stands and scrambles up the hill.

"Other side," the ride attendant says, eyes vacant, bending to reach for a curly-haired girl who'd only peeled off one shoe. Gary sees the teenager as some sort of zombie attendant of the gate into the Netherworld, Hell or Hades or something like that. Gary inhales a cloud of odor from the expanding pile of footwear that the parents kneel into, shoulders smashing one another as they sift the smelly heap for their kid's sneakers, only to give up when the reek grows too strong, turning from simple sock-sweat to dense, rotten organ gas. It makes Gary think of the World War Two documentary again. The Nazi soldiers piled up the shoes in one huge mountain after they took them from the Jewish prisoners, just before they marched them into the gas chambers. A lot of the same shoes were now piled in display cases at Auschwitz that tourists could look in at.

"Leave the shoes," Gary says. "The kids aren't coming back." A couple of the parents scrounging through the shoe piles look up at him but say nothing. Minnesotans don't confront babbling loonies unless the loonies start asking for gas money or smokes. It's best to leave the shoes there, Gary thinks. There are no children to put them back onto anyway.

"The inflatables are gobbling up the kids," Gary says, to no one in particular, but still stays in line with Peter, and they're at the front now, looking at the teenager with the blank eyes. Gary watches children disappear over the first hill and their parents move from the line and walk behind the obstacle course, over duct-taped power cords and vomit, reappearing with pale cheeks and the long stares of soldiers.

Liz will be back with popcorn, or cotton candy, or whatever, but it will be too late. Peter bounces up and down, or more or less vibrates, trying to see the entrance past the adults. Gary nudges the back of Peter's neck, his fingernail lightly scraping across his nape, signaling the boy that he can now move forward, and he drops to the gym mat to remove his shoes. Gary realizes this is something he needs to do. There's no way out.

"Is this some kind of sacrifice?" he says to the attendant.

"Four tickets," the teenager says back.

Gary hands the attendant the tickets and then leans toward him and says, "Where do we pick up the kids? Seriously. This is going too far here."

Peter throws his tennis shoes into the pile and bounces on his heels, waiting for the attendant to let him charge up the ramp.

"They go up over the top," the teenager says, windmilling his right arm and with its momentum turning away from Gary and stopping, then bending down and picking up Peter from the shoe-removal pad. He grips Peter on both sides of his rib cage and hoists him through the arch. Gary lunges for his son but misses. It's too late. His arms enclose the air, almost in slow-motion, like a dramatic movie ending. He falls to his knees on the green mat. The other parents stand there with hands on hips. They look down at him and sigh.

Liz walks up behind Gary, Heather in hand. Peter is climbing away into the distance.

"I can't find any cotton candy," Liz says. "Can you believe that?"

Gary stands and pulls Liz close and says in her ear, his voice shaking, "Go around behind the ride and see where the kids are getting off this fucking thing. Then come back and tell me. I'll wait here and try to keep my eye on him."

"You do it," she says. "I'm tired of walking."

Gary doesn't move.

"Sir, can you please step away so other people can get on the ride?" the attendant says in a flat tone.

"I swear to God I'm going to charge up that fucker," Gary says to Liz. Then he looks to his left and sees a security guard moving toward him, shoulders back and hips swaying. And then he sees the fifteen-foot-tall Army man. It thunders down a crowded aisle, clearing a path through fathers hoisting kids onto their backs and nudging aside fat mothers with its own, bigger, air-filled thighs. The inflatable army man shakes when he walks, the body bouncing six inches on the vertical like a soft shock absorber, and Gary hears it say, "I will make your children love me." He thinks he hears it say that.

"Army guy!" Heather screams.

Gary wants to inform the inflatable recruiting tool that if this kids' fest achieves its goal, there will be no children left to recruit. The children are being gobbled up. Maybe the Army man can help him rescue the children, but Gary knows it's just a blow-up doll with a little sweating human inside who's making minimum wage. He wants to lay down and sleep.

Liz grabs Gary's arm and pulls him away from the ride entrance, and at the same time, Peter, sweating and grinning, is running to the shoe pile from the other side. He straps on his tennis shoes, spots Liz and Gary, and runs over to them. He'd made it through the inflatable course in less than a minute.

"That sucked," Peter says. "Can I go again?"

Gary wanted to break into tears and hug his boy and at the same time wanted to tell him to go fuck himself for not appreciating the work he and his mom went through to get him to Fun-Fest only to hear him complain, and that didn't make him feel too good about himself.

On the drive home, Liz steers the brown Plymouth minivan with an upright, commanding posture, her left hand rubbing her swelled belly. Heather and Peter are sleeping in their car seats in the back. Liz points to a yellow grocery store marquee with black letters that reads "Ignorence is bliss." Liz loves suburban marquees. "They spelled 'ignorance' wrong," she says. "That's almost clever."

"I can't think," Gary says.

"You can think fine," she said. "You just don't."

Gary's adam's apple contracts. He tucks his thumb behind the seat belt at his breastbone and pushes out, allowing it to loosen and then tighten over his chest. "Why would you say I don't think?"

She reaches over and slaps his thigh.

He shuts his eyes and absorbs the thrum of wheels on pavement. The kids' breathing issues from the back seat. Peter's short breaths sound like the puffs of steam from a vaporizer.

Gary glances back at Peter in his car seat. His chin rests on his chest, head cocked forward.

"Sounds like Peter's not breathing too good," Gary says.

"He's fine."

"Hey, Peter," he says, reaching back to grab the boy's ankles. He gives a shake but the legs only quiver and Peter's eyes stay closed, his breathing paused.

"Pull over, Liz."

"Stop it," she says. "He's fine."

Gary's legs twitch when Peter's head snaps up. He looks at Gary with red, glossy eyes, and so Gary turns back around, closes his eyes and sleeps, the side of his head knocking against the passenger window.

Peckers

Lately, my sixth-grade son Danny has been drawing boobs and peckers on his class assignments. My wife Liz brings home one of Danny's construction paper artworks with a Post-It note attached by the teacher that says, "Please re-enforce the message that this imagery is inappropriate." The imagery appears to be a set of testicles with a giant phallus pointing straight down. I could argue to Mrs. Olson that an archetype is working through Danny, but I don't. One of my work-crews roofed her house last summer. Instead, I write on the return note, "Sure, okay," because Liz says she can't deal with this embarrassment. She volunteers in Danny's class on Tuesdays. Danny says the picture is of a coyote riding a unicycle.

"Do you really think it's a unicycle, Gary?" Liz says in bed that night. She's reading a book called *Easy Scrapbooking: The Complete Guide to Super Scrapbooking in Just 10 Minutes a Day* while I'm trying to pretend I'm sleeping so I can get back up once Liz is asleep and have a cocktail on the deck and listen to the coyotes at the edge of the development.

"Where is he getting these behaviors?" she says.

"Not from me," I say. "I don't even have a nudie magazine in the house. I can't even remember what my balls look like."

"That's sick."

"It sure is."

Liz sighs and flips a page in her oversized book. "I'm forming an official scrapbooking club. We rented space at the church."

"You mean you have to pay?"

Not only is my son a pervert, but now Liz tells me she's organizing an "official" scrapbooking club from her loose band of church and neighborhood friends.

"What do you think?" she says.

All I can think to say is, "I need to pressure-wash the camper this weekend."

"Why?"

"I don't know. We only used it once. Maybe we need to use it again."

"Did you know there's a Scrapbooking Designers Guild?" she says. "I wonder if I should get our club into it." She sighs. "I already feel so overwhelmed." She sighs again. Liz sighs all the time, long, lugubrious sighs that burrow under my skin. She sighs when a kid's sock is inside-out, a jacket slides off a coat hook, when lettuce fragments fall to the floor while she's chopping a salad, when she realizes there's no more butter, when I say "What?" after she asks me something, when Danny won't leave the TV to come eat at the table, when I say I have a work meeting. The first time I used the pressure washer, I cleaned the siding, and then I power-washed my Skeeter bass boat, which didn't need washing since I'd only used it twice. Same with the thirty-foot RV trailer parked behind the garage, a 2008 Gulf Stream Prairie Schooner I bought used for $57,000. I can't remember why I bought it. Liz sighed when I bought the boat. She sighed even more when I bought the RV.

Before Danny started his drawings and Liz started scrapbooking, I stayed at work until 6 p.m. for fifteen years. Every morning, I nodded to employees, walked upstairs to my office and logged into the computer and played games like Windows Pinball or Solitaire. Some people brag about being self-made. Not me. When I was a semester away from an MA in Psychology, my dad's liver started turning his eyeballs yellow, so he retired and turned over control of his truss-construction and roofing company and I dropped out of college before finishing my thesis, my working title of which was, *Loss of Control: Eating in Obese Adolescents.* I was a fat kid. Now I'm a fat adult. I love Kentucky Fried Chicken and Chipotle. And Dad didn't die for another twenty years. He watched TV instead, drank milk thistle tea, and organized his garage.

I spent my first two years at Wiegard Truss and Roofing firing people. The older employees hated me, but I was a good manager. I could tell who'd work and who wouldn't. Once I had the right people under me, I had nothing to do except be at the Christmas party to pass out bonus checks and tell bad jokes into the ballroom microphone. Still, I always put in my office time and the plant manager often drops by to show me numbers, and we pretend I understand them. In the meantime, I sit at the computer and play games or bid on eBay items. Last week, I bought a new depth-finder for my Skeeter even though the old one apparently works. I also bought a two-man tent. I hope to use both items some day.

Today, though, I log off the computer when I get a call from Danny's principal, Gabriel Abraham. He says, "Mr. Wiegard, would it be possible to have a meeting on this issue of Danny's? We're not *overly* concerned. We're just concerned."

"Sure," I say, "you want me to come by this afternoon?"

"I'm sure you're busy. We can schedule an appointment."

"I'm not busy," I say, and tell my secretary Marlys that I'm going to the Chipotle for lunch.

I walk out to my SUV, a brand-new 2010 Lincoln Aviator, and think about driving to the Badlands. It's only a twelve hour drive. Instead, though, I drive to Michael's craft store and buy Liz a leather-bound scrapbook and some Looney Tunes stickers for the photos of Danny when he was little. He liked Bugs Bunny best. I like Wile E. Coyote. Liz wrote her college thesis on the effects of psychotropic drugs on children of differing socio-economic classes, and then she took a job teaching at KinderCare. In ten years, she's worked her way up from Assistant Program Director to Lead Program Director. She had more time to devote to work once our oldest kids, Heather and Peter, left the house and she only had Danny to grapple with. Maybe scrapbooking will help her stop sighing so much.

Next, I go to B. Dalton's bookstore at the mall and look for something on how to deal with kids who draw peckers on their homework. I tell this to the clerk, a kid with a beaded necklace and dreadlocks, and after a silent moment, he says I should scout through dream interpretation books. I pick up a copy of Carl Jung's *Symbols of Transformation*, which I'd read back in college. I look in the index and find "phallus" on page 97. It says the phallus is "the source of life and libido, the creator and worker of miracles, and as such it is worshipped everywhere." I could make this argument to administration, that Danny's pecker-drawing is a miracle, when I get to the school, but the peckers aren't the only issue. Our last name is Wiegard, and Danny has been writing his name on his papers as Danny W., and scribbling dots on each descender of the "W", making the letter look like boobs. According to Jung, breasts represent life, the earth mother, provider. He says that in Egypt, a man could seek immortality by sucking the breasts of a goddess. You can't do that sort of thing in a third-ring suburb, though.

"Inappropriate," I tell Danny once we're gathered in the principal's office. I'm clenching my fists on the chair rails in front of Principal Abraham's desk. "This is really offensive to people." His teacher, Mrs. Olson, is also there. Her eyebrows are close together. She's standing by Abraham and wearing narrow eyeglasses with a neck chain like a 1950s schoolmarm even though it's 2010. Danny looks down and rubs his hands together as if he's washing them.

"Do you understand how someone might be offended?" I say to him, playing to the script.

"Sure," he says. "Okay."

"I really appreciate you coming in, Mr. Wiegard," Principal Abraham says to me. "Danny, you can go back to class now. And thank you, Mrs. Olson."

I stand to leave.

"May I speak with you alone for a minute, Mr. Wiegard?"

"Sure," I say. "Okay."

When Mrs. Olson and Danny leave, Principal Abraham sits on the front corner of his desk, rests his hands on one knee and says, "I'm really sorry about all this, Jerry."

"Gary."

"Listen, there's nothing unusual about what Danny did here. It happens frequently, but some are more sensitive than others, so that's what we have to deal with here." He winks as though we share some sort of male covenant, and for the first time, I notice that he's black. I've never noticed a black person in our suburb of thirty thousand, except for an adopted kid named Dustin who plays on Danny's baseball team.

"It's no problem," I say. "I was on my way to Chipotle anyway."

"Pardon?" says the principal.

"Chipotle. It's kind of a fast-food gourmet Mexican restaurant."

"What I mean is, what does Chipotle have to do with what I just said?"

Behind Principal Abraham on a hutch is a 5x7 framed picture of him and his family smiling in front of the giant Epcot Center golf ball. The real name of the golf ball is something like "Spaceship Earth," which means there must be some sort of space-ride inside. We have the same picture of the huge golf ball in the background, with Liz and me and Peter and Heather standing, and Danny in a stroller, grouped in the same place as the principal's family, right in front of the entrance to the amusement park.

"I took the family to Disney World when Danny was a baby," I say, gesturing to the photo. "We bought some time-share points. I don't remember anything except that I was tired all the time." For no reason, I'm smiling. I shake Principal Abraham's hand and crave a burrito with a huge dollop of sour cream.

I exit the office at 3:00 after going onto eBay and bidding on a green double-burner Coleman camp stove like I had in college, and then I let the truck idle in the parking lot. I stare at the leather-bound scrapbook and my Carl Jung book on the passenger seat. One of the books lies atop the other. It must mean something. The second-shift workers drive in and some of them wave at me as I unzip my slacks.

The cars pass from the street to the administrative lot, where I'm parked, and then disappear through a gate into the truss-construction facility out back. Since I sit up high in my Aviator, there is no danger of passing employees seeing my pecker. I can still wave, too, because I'm not masturbating, nor am I erect. I'm just pushing in my gut with my left hand, waving with my right, and looking at my penis, which I haven't studied for years. It arcs loosely over my zipper and sprawls on my slacks like a drunken partygoer passed out on a couch.

When I get home, Liz is opening and closing kitchen cabinets, and when she sees me, she scolds me for always unloading the dishwasher when the plastic containers and cups are still wet. I tell her I haven't unloaded the dishwasher for weeks, and she says she's not surprised by that. Danny sits at the kitchen table looking down and rubbing his hands together over his chubby belly.

"Do you want to ask your son what he did after your meeting today?" Liz puts her hands on her hips and sighs.

"No," I say, and walk back out the front door and into the SUV. I want to drive to the Badlands and bark at the moon, but instead, I drive to Bill's Small Engine where I bought my air-compressor.

"What can I do you for?" Bill asks. He wears a black baseball cap with yellow lettering that says *DeWalt*.

"I need an attachment."

"How's the compressor working for you?"

"Good," I say. Also, I could tell Bill that I just ran out on my family, and now I need to drive home and eat dinner or this could be the end, but instead I say, "I'm thinking about getting a new pressure washer attachment."

"What's wrong with the old one?"

"I don't know."

I walk back into the house with my head down. The scrapbook still sits on the passenger seat of the Lincoln. It's been an hour since I left, and when I return, Liz is still banging around the kitchen and Danny is still slouching at the table and rubbing his hands together. Now, though, he's got a bunch of drawings in front of him.

"He did it again," Liz says, igniting the gas range like I was never gone. We have mostly Maytag appliances. "Your little meeting sure helped a lot."

I sit at the table. "Inappropriate," I say, fanning out the evidence. "I want no more nipples on your Ws, Danny."

"Gary," says Liz, laying a cutting block on the counter, "this isn't funny."

"I know it's not," I say. "All I'm saying is that there are certain things we can't do in certain places." My eyes get hot. "Right, Danny?"

"Sure," he says, looking down, and for the first time, I notice how Danny's pudgy, swelled face is full of freckles and bright pink zits, dense and compressed like a rash. He squints up at me for a second but can't focus on my face. His eyeballs float from side to side like he's trying not to look into the sun. I want to get in the truck and drive with my hazards on all the way to South Dakota. I want my son to look me in the eyes. I want him to see me for once.

"Danny, I'm really serious about this. It has to stop." I can't make my voice rise and fall anymore.

"I can't help it," he says. "I'm bored."

"There is no excuse for this behavior," says Liz. "Tell him, Dad."

"I just did. I don't know what else to say."

"Me neither," says Danny.

Before dinner, I go into the bathroom and as I'm leaning over the sink with my face six inches from the mirror checking my nose hairs and the trim around my goatee—I'm one of those middle-aged graying guys with a goatee—Liz walks up behind me and says, "You need to spend more time with Danny. Why don't you take him into work tomorrow so you can show him what you do for a living."

"What do I do for a living?"

"Maybe that's the problem."

In the evening, Liz reads to Danny while I go out on the deck to watch the tree line and listen for the coyotes that roam a stretch of woods and the vacant fields that border the edge of our cul de sac development, just west of the under-construction community center that will have an indoor waterslide with a tropical theme—plastic palm trees, rubber coconuts, cabanas, the whole bit— and workout rooms. I sit on a deck chair and listen over our backyard to the yips that skate the neighborhood, bouncing between houses. It sounds like a dozen coyotes roaming the edges of the development taunting the kenneled dogs, but two or three coyotes can sound like twenty.

Once, when Liz and I were in the Badlands, before we had kids, we took a hike but went too far and couldn't get back to the campground before dark, so as we stumbled back, we walked into a dried up creek bed that we knew was the last obstacle between us and the campground, and we couldn't find a way up the other side. The creek wall was ten feet high with no grooves. Coyotes started yipping. The voices bounced around the creek bed, tunneled and echoing, sounding like hundreds of crazed dogs running toward us. Liz scrambled for the wall, fingers digging into sandstone, and she clawed her way up like Spiderman and ran across the meadow to the lantern lights of the campground. She didn't scream or sigh. She was lovely when she was afraid of something that mattered.

The Aurora Borealis's green gases squiggle fuzzily over the yellow suburban lights. The coyotes yip and seem close. I walk down and lie on the lawn and look up at the Northern Lights. The green gases are a veil and the dim stars behind it are freckles and zits.

From inside the house, I hear, "Are you going to be up all night again?"

I walk upstairs to Danny's room. I squeeze his chubby shoulder and he rolls onto his back and squints up at me with red eyes like he's been crying. I sit on the edge of his bed and tell him a coyote story. I tell him that in 1987, a coyote sat on a butte in the Badlands and stared up at the slowly arcing moon. The Badlands Moon, when full, looked like a shiny hunk of quartz. The Badlands Moon, when full, smiled from lunar ear to lunar ear. The

Badlands Moon, when full, looked like a large cup of floating ice-water, ready to tip. But it never did. From horizon to horizon, the coyote craned its head and licked and nipped at the full, moist, celestial body. Every night for three days, he returned and sat, and licked and nipped, until the sky clouded up.

"I don't know how the story ends," I say.

"Okay," Danny whispers. He closes his eyes.

"Wait, I remember the ending," I tell him. "It started to rain real hard and the moon disappeared and the wind started blowing hard, so we packed up camp and drove to a motel in Wall, about twenty minutes away. Then we went to Wall Drug the next day and ate at a huge buffet."

"What about the coyote?"

"Good question."

When I'm done with the story, I smoke a cigarette on the deck and listen to the barking of a pit bull down at the end of the cul de sac. The sliding door cracks open and Liz says, "You gonna be up all night again?"

I don't want the pecker to be a stick figure on a unicycle. I want it to be a stick figure atop an amazing pecker. I want the stick figure to be amazed by how huge it is, how he swings his legs over its side, running in space like a cockroach pinned to a board, and all because of this amazingly large pecker.

"I'll be right in," I say, and I am. I lie in bed and listen to Liz sigh in her sleep, and stare up into the plaster, but then the light clicks on and Liz sits up and says, "I'm reading for awhile. Go sleep on the couch if you have to."

She pulls her book, *Easy Scrapbooking: The Complete Guide to Super Scrapbooking in Just 10 Minutes a Day*, off of her nightstand.

"Maybe I'll read, too," I say. "I got a book today." I don't mention the leather-bound scrapbook still sitting on the passenger seat of the SUV.

"What?" She creases her eyebrows and sets her book on her lap. "Why are you reading all of the sudden?" I tell her about my visit to B. Dalton's and she says, "It sounds like you acted like a parent today."

"Listen," I say, my voice rising. "Remember that class we took on counseling methods our senior year? Remember the Jungian analysis part?"

"No."

"Sure you do. The archetypes, remember? The dream symbols? Listen, the breasts in Danny's drawing are not any particular boobs. They're everyone's. He has archetypes working through him. He can't help it."

"You're talking crazy."

"Boobs, peckers, coyotes. They're connected."

"What are you talking about?"

"Never mind."

Liz flips another page in her book on scrapbooking. "I can't believe we were fed that garbage in college. What were we thinking?"

"We were *thinking*."

"What?"

The curtain drifts into the room through the open window as a breeze picks up outside. I put my book back on my nightstand. "I got a new pressure washer nozzle today."

"What was wrong with the old one?"

"I don't know."

I close my eyes and listen through the open bedroom window for coyotes, for the yips getting closer. In my imagination, I stare into the darkness of the woods. Beyond the darkness, more blackness, and the yips dance from tree to tree as though the animals are running in circles.

"I think we've repressed Danny," Liz says as she reads. "That's what his problem is. Maybe you're accidentally right with this archetype stuff." Her theory is that we've been throwing blankets over TV screens, towels over body parts, and jumping for volume controls so much that he's wondering what we're hiding, and so maybe his collective unconscious is coughing up the answers: boobs and peckers. We keep doors locked when we bathe or shower, and we only mate once every two months, late on weekend nights when Danny is sleeping, and we each give the act half-attention because our ears are trained to the floor above where Danny's room is.

"We need to talk more to Danny," Liz says. "We're hiding too much from him. We need to be more open."

"Like Amsterdam," I say into the pillow.

"What?"

"The Amsterdam stereotype," I say, though I really want to tell her that Carl Jung says that the "phallus often stands for creative divinity," but I'm trying to pretend I'm going to sleep so I can get back up again and go outside once Liz is asleep.

"We should go camping this weekend," I say, but I

don't mean to say it out loud.

"I have scrapbooking at the church on Saturday, remember? It's our first time renting out a space, Gary."

Once Liz is sleeping, I walk out to the truck and grab the leather-bound scrapbook from the passenger's seat. In the basement office, I lay the scrapbook on the carpet, open it to the first page and start digging through white plastic bins containing rubber stamps, stickers, scissors, ribbon, colored paper, glue, glitter, laminate, and baby wipes to clean the rubber stamps, and I create a collage of images from piles of magazines such as *Outside* and *Redbook*. I set my digital camera to the close-up setting and take a couple of photos of my erection, the first I've had in months. I load the photos through FireWire into my computer and print out color copies. When I'm done cutting, pasting, drawing and writing, I place the book in a bin, underneath the scrapbook Liz is currently working on, titled "The Birthday Boy," about Danny's various birthday parties. She's scrapbooking the parties by theme rather than chronology since Danny's birthdays have all been managed by themes: *Thomas the Tank Engine*, *Toy Story*, *Scooby Doo*, *Star Wars*, whatever merchandise was front and center in the Wal-Mart party section at the time.

Saturday evening, Liz loads her bins into her minivan and heads to the church. I walk upstairs to Danny's room and knock.

"What?" he says. I can tell from his muffled tone that he's not facing the door.

"Can I come in?"

"Why?"

I hear repetitive electronic music and pinging noises, the sounds of Xbox.

"Open the door. I have an idea I want to run by you."

"What?"

"Open the door. Let's take a hike into the woods."

"Why?"

As the sun dips into the earth, I stand in the backyard and stare into the woods until they go black. Beyond the forest, which is a quarter-mile deep, is a field of upturned dirt being smoothed out for a community center. As I walk into the darkness, I imagine that no more buildings will be built here. This is where the coyotes run around. I want Danny to walk out here with me, but he won't unlock his door. He's playing *Rampage*. And I imagine, just as I get to other edge of the woods and stare into the black field, that Liz notices the new scrapbook at the bottom of the bin. She's in the church basement, her friend Laura sitting to one side and her friend Nancy on the other at a long table. Her eyes spring wide for a second when she sees a yellow coyote with an erect pecker riding a unicycle across the first page. Then I imagine that she smiles.

Swimming

On the flight to Tampa, Gary got separated from his wife and son. The seat the clerk assigned him was four rows back from Liz and Danny. The flight attendant asked Gary if he wanted to sit up in an open first-class seat instead, for his trouble. He said "Sure" in a flat tone, but Liz knew what he was thinking. He was thinking that if he didn't have to sit with his wife and kid, he could order a Bloody Mary without getting leered at or sighed at. And he could take a nap. He'd been taking a lot of naps lately. A week earlier, his secretary Marlys had found him in a fetal ball on his office floor and dialed 911. By the time the paramedics arrived, he'd rolled to his back and was snoring, and all Marlys could say was, "I'm so embarrassed. He usually naps on the couch." This time he didn't make it that far.

As the plane taxied to the runway, small TV screens folded down from the ceiling like robots to show the safety video. The head stewardess announced over the speakers that once they reached cruise altitude, anyone who paid two dollars could watch a Catherine Zeta-

Jones movie. A romantic comedy didn't interest Gary or Liz, though.

Danny had on his ear buds hooked to his iPod, loaded with gothic death metal, at least that's how Gary and Liz understood Danny's preferred musical genre.

"It's not goth," Danny once said. "It's speed-metal."

"Oh, like Metallica," said Gary, trying to "connect."

"Metallica is weak," said Danny.

Gary waved his hands in the air and said "Fuck it."

Liz looked out the window as the plane surged forward. Airplane hangars and warehouses and office buildings became a single dark line that dropped from view. In the middle of ascent, the engines humming like a dishwasher, Liz pulled the inflight magazine from the pouch on the back of the seat in front of her and smiled at the picture of an older Donny and Marie grinning warmly at her—they were performing in a Las Vegas show—and wondered if the 767 went into a dive, would Gary unbuckle and rush back to be with his wife and son or would he freeze, his hands clenched to the armrests, and stare into the back of the seat in front of him? Would Gary be a hero like the fathers and husbands on the Sunday night made-for-TV movies or would he freeze up and piss his pants?

They didn't crash.

When Liz and Danny walked off the plane, Gary stood in the concourse. He had his bag over his shoulder and leaned against a post. Liz smelled the vapor on his breath and said, "You and Danny get the luggage and I'll go find the rent-a-car place. I'll meet you at the baggage claim."

Two days before they left, Gary's mother Carol called. Liz answered with the speaker-phone at the kitchen bar so Gary could hear from the living room. He lay on the couch watching a documentary about migratory birds.

"Vicki just called," Carol said. Vicki was Carol's twin sister who lived in Florida. "She went into the doctor to check on some back pain from playing tennis and they found a tumor on her spine."

"Is it cancerous?" Liz said.

"It's already got branches."

Carol was a retired nurse, so she knew what "branches" meant. Liz didn't. She wanted to ask, but she also wanted to wait for Gary to say something because Vicki was *his* aunt, not hers. Gary didn't say anything. The only noise from the living room was a bird from the TV that half-twittered like it wasn't sure about something.

"What part of the spine?" Liz finally said.

"Lower," Carol said. "She's going on hospice. She refused treatment."

"I'm so sorry, Carol."

"Oh well. Vicki always did what she wanted. Why should now be any different?"

Liz walked around the kitchen bar so she could see Gary. He lay stomach-down on the couch, left arm hanging down to the carpet. He rolled his head over the edge of the cushion and looked down at his hand and started counting his fingers.

"You'll have to give us Vicki's number," Liz said. "We'll have to visit her when we're down there."

Gary continued to count his fingers.

Vicki was a mythical figure to Liz even though they'd only met once. Just after their oldest kid, Heather, was born, twenty-one years earlier, Vicki and her husband Jack were in town staying with Gary's folks, and they came to the house, the Orrin Thompson rambler starter home Gary and Liz bought right out of college. Vicki wore a red golf visor and a flowery tennis skirt over tanned legs. She had an unlit cigarette in her fingers and a silver tooth in the upper left that made her smile glint.

Liz handed Heather to her, and Vicki sat on the couch with the baby on her lap. "He looks fine," she said, inspecting Heather through a squint. She looked under her armpits.

"'She.' It's a 'she,'" Gary said.

"What?" said Jack.

"It's not a *he*," said Gary, bringing in a gin tumbler to pour some rounds. "It's a *she*. Aunt Vicki said *he*."

"Whatever it is," Jack said, "it's got good size."

"Precious," Carol said.

"They grow up fast," Jack said. "Before you know it, he'll be taking the car out without your permission."

"*She*," said Liz.

Then Aunt Vicki said, "My god, babies are awful."

Liz leaned forward and almost said, "What a horrible thing to say," but she didn't. Vicki held Heather upright on her lap and leaned forward, Heather's face a foot from her own. Her little baby lips puckered like she had to poop.

"God, remember the crying, Jack?" Vicki said. "And you always had to keep your eyes on them. Hated cooking all the time, too. Never any time for yourself." She smiled at Liz, her tooth glinting. "I've got four grown children and love them with a purple passion, but I could have done without the little-kid part."

Carol cleared her throat.

"Just get used to being tired all the time, Liz," Vicki said. "You'll make life easier on yourself." She handed Heather across the coffee table to Liz and said, "Beautiful baby. No kidding." Heather's head lolled as Liz took her back.

Two decades and three kids later, Liz got Vicki's point, even though Liz had become the Director of a KinderCare facility. Still, she never had much direct contact with the toddlers at work. Instead, the kids she mostly babysat were the employees, who were mostly gum-popping teenagers who used to make ten bucks an hour babysitting neighborhood kids when they were thirteen—parking the kids in front of DVD players and loading them up with crackers so they could spend their time texting their girl and boyfriends—and now they thought they were qualified to actively engage and nurture dozens of toddlers at a time, for durations of eight to ten hours. They weren't. And Liz had to deal with them. Liz had to replace them with new unqualified interviewees when they didn't show up for their next shift. Liz had to deal with their parents when they called and said their teenage girls were overworked and that their job was making them cry sometimes. These were the "toddlers" Liz dealt with, and then when she got off work—she often stayed late, alone in her office, after the kids had all been picked up—she had to take care of more infants: a brooding adolescent and a miserable husband. Her oldest son Peter had just moved out, at least, and Heather was off at college and seemed to have her life together.

Now, whenever Liz looked in mirrors at the dark patches like bruises underneath her eyes, she heard Vicki's voice. Once, when their third-born, Danny, was four and vandalized his room because he didn't want to go to bed, Liz said to Gary, "Maybe your aunt was right." But that was the only time she said it out loud. Otherwise, she accepted her paychecks and fulfilled her domestic mothering duties. She punched in, and she stayed punched in.

Liz booked the Florida trip because all Gary did was drink, sleep and watch TV. And Danny lived life in ear buds and in *World of Warcraft* where he was a "Rogue with subtlety skills." His special skill was to give opponents hemorrhages. Giving enemies brain hemorrhages was considered a "subtle" skill. Liz's job was to bring her boys back into life, to make them visible to each other, to herself. And she had to tell Gary about the baby in controlled conditions. She needed to fix things. Gary had also just turned forty-three, which gave him another reason to sleep. She told Gary one night while she made dinner and he flipped through the mail, "Listen, if you turn forty-four, that means you *made* it to forty-four.

That's a good thing."

He shrugged. And then she showed him a book called *Listening to Midlife: Turning Your Crisis into a Quest*. He just looked at the title and said, mouth hung open like a stroke patient, "Let's go see the mermaids then. I get the idea."

"What idea?"

"The idea you're going after. I don't need to read the book. I get the idea."

He walked into the living room with a Michelob Golden Light in a bottle, lay on the couch and watched a cable show about a wilderness survivalist who ate raw salmon and shit berries.

Liz drove the rental car from the Tampa Airport to Kissimmee in the dark. She chose a purple PT Cruiser just to see what Gary would say, but like he knew she wanted him to say something, he just said, "Nice car," and threw his bag in the back. She couldn't tell if he was being facetious. They had a time-share condominium at a place called the Vacation Villas five miles from the Disney entrance. They had bought their package when they were on their honeymoon back in 1996, two years before they had Heather, and got roped into a four-hour long presentation. Liz wanted to buy two weeks of time per year, which is also what the oily-haired salesman Carlos wanted. As they sat at the "closing table" in a large cafeteria full of vacationers getting "closed," Gary turned red-faced and sarcastic, but he was hungover and wanted to get out of the presentation, so he signed a one-week-a-year deal with RPI that dealt in "points" that they could trade based on their "home base" at Vacation Villas for various resorts all over the planet, depending on color, all of which Gary could understand but not articulate, and his hands had quivered so bad that he had to trust that Liz knew what she was doing. Though they never traveled to any foreign countries in the subsequent twenty-three years, they used to fly down to Florida when all the kids were smaller and together, but they hadn't used any of their points for the past three years, and the oldest kids, Heather, twenty-one, and Peter, nineteen, were out of the nest and now it was just Gary and Liz and fourteen-year-old Danny, who didn't want to come because it would be lame, so Liz had to use the "It's a law that we can't leave you home" rhetoric on him.

As Liz drove out of Tampa, Gary snored in the passenger seat and Danny stared forward, spacing out, his ear buds implanted. Liz could hear the tinny noises. Danny liked a band called Suffocation that "sang" scream-metal. Liz pushed the button and brought down her window just a crack for the Florida smell, brine-filled oxygen from the ocean, moist and warm. It was thick, like food, and the hiss of the dashboard fan and the outside air almost put Liz to sleep.

An hour into the drive, Gary coughed and woke up. He looked out at the dark of billboards and shadowy shapes of gnarled trees. "I need a goddamn coffee," he said.

Liz pulled into a 7-Eleven. Gary grunted out the door, stood in the lot and reached for his toes to stretch his hamstrings, but his hands only reached his knees because of his belly. He walked inside, and five minutes later, returned with a six pack.

"I love Florida," he said, and wiped a slick of sweat from his forehead. "Where else can a guy get a six pack of Bass Ale at midnight on a Monday?"

"I thought you wanted coffee."

"I changed my fucking mind."

Once they checked into the suite at the resort, Liz set her bag on the bedroom floor. She turned on the ceiling fan, opened the patio door a crack to let in air and walked out into the main room to see if Gary and Danny were situated.

"You guys alright?" she said. "I'm going to bed."

Danny lay on the couch and Gary sat on a stool at the kitchenette bar, drinking Bass Ale and watching TV. Neither of them answered Liz. The voice on the TV talked about purported UFO evidence in the Puget Sound area in the form of metal fragments that fell from a crashing spaceship.

In the morning, Gary sat on a stool drinking coffee and reading a brochure about the Burt Reynolds and Friends Museum. He thought about the time when he was younger and saw Burt Reynolds and Dom DeLuise having an improvised pie fight on Johnny Carson's *Tonight Show*. He turned to tell Danny but the kid wouldn't have got it, so he sat there like an idiot, his smile disappearing, the brochure quivering in his fingers. He wore a tan and red button-down short-sleeve shirt with white orchids on it. Danny snoozed on the couch, still in his black jeans and a white t-shirt that read, *I AM the American Dream.*

"We should call Vicki," Liz said. She reached down and shook Danny's shoulder. "Get up. Let's get breakfast."

"I'll call her," Gary said. His face was swollen. "She's *my* aunt."

Instead, they drove to the Magic Kingdom. When they got there, they parked and rode a little train pulled by a golf cart into the turnstiles where they bought tickets and then climbed onto the monorail that coiled them around a lake and through the inside of a hotel and then dropped them at the park entrance. After they floated with the stream of people through the main gate, Danny took a seat on a bench on Main Street USA, huffing and red-faced, and said, "This is bullshit."

"Inappropriate," Liz said. "Gary, tell him he can't talk like that."

"You can't talk like that."

"I need a salted pretzel," Danny said.

"You need a lot of things."

"Stop it," Liz said. "We're here to have fun. Let's have fun."

Gary put his head down and walked into the mass of moving bodies. Danny and Liz followed. Gary's armpits squirted sweat into his shirt. They got in line for The Pirates of the Caribbean ride, which Danny wanted to see because he read on the Internet that Jack Sparrow from the movies had been built into the attraction.

After twenty minutes, Danny said, "I don't want to wait. My ankle bones hurt."

He talked in monotone, didn't look at Gary or Liz, didn't take out his ear buds. He stared at the ground and held his hands on his stomach like he had the flu. Gary folded his arms across his chest and stared up at a thin white cloud. Then, his red forehead spackled in sweat-beads, he stared down at Danny and opened his mouth to say something.

"Don't start," Liz said, so Gary asked a man standing in line, "Do they serve beer at this park?" The man shook his head no, his face redder than Gary's, but the stranger looked sunburned rather than full of suppressed rage. Liz folded her arms and wondered when Gary would explode, and how, and then she stared at the hip pack squeezed between his stomach and thigh and realized that she'd married a man who wore a hip pack and meant it.

"I have to go to the bathroom," she said, and left the line.

After their trip to the Magic Kingdom, they decided to just lay around the resort pool the next day instead of seeing the mermaids or Gary's dying aunt Vicki. By noon, Danny was still on the couch playing video games, and Liz was swimming around drunk in the resort pool. At first, Gary swam a bit with her, but then Liz got preoccupied with trying to get a little retarded girl to float in an inner tube and so Gary laid back in a deck chair and put his forearm over his eyes. The girl's grandfather stood behind the little girl on the steps and held her by the hands and dipped her down to her bony hips. When he tried to bring her down another step and the water reached her belly, she moaned. Liz swam over with one of the blue inner tubes that the resort provided and swimmers fought over because there were more of them than the tubes, and said, "You want to float on this, honey? It's fun."

The girl's teeth were big and always showed, like she was smiling all the time, but her face was just frozen that way, and what made Gary nervous was that Liz was buzzed on wine, his own fault for bringing cups down to the pool so early, and she wanted that retarded girl to float. It was like an obsession for Liz. The girl's arms and legs were thin like tent poles, her knees and elbows swelled and reddish like an arthritic's, and her mouth and jutting jaw took up half of her face. She looked like Karen Carpenter in her starving days, all teeth and cheekbones. Liz had a soft spot for kids and retards and people with disabilities, which was why she managed a corporate daycare center—and, she joked, her toddler husband and son—and so when Gary saw her get in her "helping others" mode, he lay back in a deck chair, sunglasses centered, one towel over his belly and one over his legs, waiting for an awkward scene, pretending not to know the buzzed lady in the pool.

"Go ahead, use the tube," Liz said. She pushed it toward the skinny grandfather.

"No thanks," he said, "She's pretty funny about that kind of stuff."

"Float, honey." Liz persisted. Then she looked at the grandfather, who toughed out a smile but didn't look back at her. "She can float," she said to him. Then she looked back into the girl's eyes. "You want to try this?"

The girl continued to bare her teeth.

"She has a thing about climbing in things," the grandfather said, voice rising a bit, "but good try."

Gary took a deep breath as Liz swam away. She climbed out of the pool and walked over to the hot tub. When Gary walked over and climbed in with her, he didn't mention anything about the girl. Instead, he said, "You having fun yet?"

Her eyes were red from chlorine.

"Are you being sarcastic?" she said.

When the three kids were little, Gary and Liz used to take them all down to Kissimmee every other winter. They'd hit the amusement parks the first couple days and then lounge around. The kids would swim and play mini-golf before ending up bored in front of the TV while Liz and Gary would sit on the pool deck and drink cold beverages and watch the stream of covered golf carts driven by guys in suits and gold jewelry circle the fence that enclosed the pool area. It was a standard route on the tour part of the mandatory time-share presentation. The people in the pool area avoided eye contact with the golf cart passengers. They understood the deal.

Before the triplicate chains of time-share and mortgage and the kids, Liz and Gary used to drive up to a resort in Northern Minnesota in the summers and actually enjoy it. They used to sit on a third floor deck that overlooked a forested river valley and play cribbage and smoke cigarettes and drink gin until it was light out. Liz always stole Gary's knobs. That's a cribbage term. They'd have sex every couple of hours. Back in those days, they rented the expensive rooms with the hot tubs in the living room.

During one of those trips, Heather was created, and then they had two more kids, which put up a wall between them for twenty years. They spent their time as activity planners, taking kids to carnivals and fairs, birthday parties, bowling lanes, baseball practice, gymnastics, guitar lessons, choir practice, water parks, amusement parks. And when they took them to resorts, one parent would take the kids to the pool while the other one got some "alone time" in the room with a beverage and some TV.

And the reason why Liz was now drunk in the pool by noon and trying to persuade a retarded girl to swim is because now both parents could go down to the pool and drink since they only had one kid along, and it was a kid who preferred to sit in the hotel room playing *World of Warcraft* on the laptop he'd brought with him. Liz had started swimming at 9 a.m. and by noon, she was tanked. When she came out of the pool, she laid back in her deck chair, put a towel over her head and watched TV on her iPhone. Gary lay next to her in a patio chair pretending to read a book called *As a Man Thinketh*, another self-help book Liz gave him. He got as far as the back of the book, which said "A person's mind is like a garden, which may be intelligently cultivated, or allowed to run wild. Either way, the garden will bring forth. You will be awed by the relevance of the author's thoughts and observations on the power of the mind, and mankind's ability to control life's outcomes by controlling what goes into it." Liz got him the book because she thought he was lethargic, or as she often said, "checked out."

So, as Gary sat by the pool and pretended to read about the garden of his mind, Liz drank white wine from a Thermos and watched a Lifetime movie on her two-inch screen about a woman running for District Attorney who gets harassed by a stalker hired by her opponent, an old white politico-type played by the guy who was the Smoking Man in the *X-Files*. With Liz's head safely under the towel, Gary could pretend to read and watch the swimming girls through his sunglasses. And right when he was reading on the back of the book that the guy who wrote all the *Chicken Soup for the Soul* books had read *As a Man Thinketh* over twenty-five times, two young ladies walked onto the pool deck and started adjusting some reclining deck chairs and peeling off their the white skirts that covered their bikinis.

One was brunette and one blonde. Both wore white two-pieces. The brunette had larger breasts than the blonde, but the blonde was better proportioned, more symmetrical. To Gary, she was slim, but not anorexic like the retarded girl, and she had a tremendous cunt. Not that he could technically see it, but he had an effective view of the white fabric hugging it tight between the thighs like a kid squeezing a teddy bear. Gary thought she noticed him looking at her through the right corner of his sunglasses because she spread her knees and touched her heels together like she was stretching her inner thigh muscles and he could see the full breadth of her pubic bone, covered of course, but nonetheless. It looked like a cliff. And then she started adjusting her top with her forefingers, reaching under her breasts to pull the bikini taut, and she had her eyes closed and she licked her lips in circles. Gary thought she was taunting him like the guy in the *Vacation* movie who drove the old station wagon cross-country, and the hot model woman would pull up in the red sports car and shake her hair at him and lick her lips, making his forehead sweat, and then she'd accelerate and he'd have to go off and masturbate alone in a cheap motel room while the kids were in the outdoor pool swimming around in leaves and grass clippings. But that's the stuff they didn't show in the movies, the old man gritting his teeth, alone in the shower, pulling on the old warhorse. Gary threw a towel over his boner as his phone rang. He plucked it out of his sandal on the ground. It was Danny, from the room.

"I'm hungry," Danny said.

"Okay," Gary said. "Thank you for sharing."

"Aren't we going to eat?"

"There's snacks in the room. Have some Chicken 'n' Biscuits or something."

"I ate them already. I want real food."

"Go get some real food then."

"I mean some hot food," Danny said. "I want something warmed up."

"We got a microwave in there, don't we?"

"You want me to microwave graham crackers? All we

got is graham crackers."

"Microwave whatever you want."

"Jesus."

"Everyone's got their own fucking garden," Gary said.
"What?"

Gary turned off his phone. He laid it on his sweating
chest. He put his hands behind his head, lifted his head
and looked down over his belly, which swelled up like
pie crust in an oven. It was reddening and smeared with
perspiration. He couldn't see his knees unless he bent his
legs, but he was suddenly too tired to do that.

Gary had told Liz yesterday while the three were having
lunch at Redd Rockett's Pizza Port in Tomorrowland
that he loved all his kids, but having another one would
probably kill him. It was one of those thoughts that came
out by accident, when he was chewing on his pizza and
looking at infants in strollers, their heads lolling to the
side like they were paralyzed.

"I can't imagine it, either," she'd said back, but she
didn't look at Gary.

He should have known something was up with his
wife, but he wasn't paying attention. Danny was up at
one of the food counters ordering an expensive ice cream
cone when they said this stuff, so he couldn't hear. When
the kids were off getting stuff was when Liz and Gary
always talked. Gary didn't really listen, though.

He made sure his sunglasses were placed so he could
look ahead at the pool but aim his pupils to the right
at the girls in the bikinis. The young women talked to
each other in Eastern European accents, tough and

jagged words: "prozce," "dobre," "pivo." Gary imagined a world in which they might seek him out to fuck him, but he also knew that even if they were weird and invited him into a three-way that included vodka and rough language, he couldn't hold up his end of the deal. He was forty-four, thirty pounds overweight for a guy who's 5' 9" tall, and perspired so excessively that his doctor actually labeled him with a condition called hyperhidrosis, which meant that he sweated a lot for no reason, and during sex, he was slithering and drippy. One time, about a decade ago, Gary and Liz went to marriage counseling, and Liz described Gary's sexual acumen as "Workmanlike. He gets the job done."

"I punch in, I punch out," Gary said.

Later in the afternoon, Gary took Danny out to dinner so that Liz could have the TV and "alone time."

"Bring me back whatever," Liz said. She slurred a bit. "I'm not hungry." She uncorked another bottle of cabernet and was already in her bathrobe.

Gary took Danny to a Black Angus restaurant and loaded him up on red meat and potato products. They said a total of nine words to each other during the whole dinner process.

"You full yet?" Gary said.

"Yeah."

"We should get going."

"Okay."

When they got back to the room with a to-go box full of dried french fries, a soggy garden salad, and a piece of chicken, Liz was snoozing on the couch, still dressed, sitting straight up. Gary helped her stand and walk to the bedroom, and when she landed on the bed, she said, "I didn't say it before, but I was pregnant for a couple of months."

She rolled onto her back and Gary pulled off her sandals. She was still in her one-piece bathing suit.

"You were what?"

"Not a biggie," she said. "I lost it anyways."

"Christ all fucking mighty."

"I figured why bother."

"Why bother what?"

"Telling anything. I lost it."

Gary dropped her legs onto the bed. They didn't bounce. They stuck there.

"Why are you telling me now then?" he said.

"Probably the wine," she said. "I had too much of it."

She rolled over onto her face and sucked in air. Since Gary couldn't ask any follow-up questions, he went into the bathroom, sat on the toilet and masturbated, not because he was horny, but because he couldn't think of what else to do. But it was nothing as complicated as the time a month earlier when he had sex with a full jar of cholesterol-free mayonnaise. He'd been working on his cholesterol level for about a year since his doctor told him that not only did he have an excessive sweating problem, but his LDL levels were too high for a middle-aged guy. But Gary hated the taste of the cholesterol-free mayonnaise because it was greasy and upset his stomach and made him fart like a Clydesdale. That's why the jar was still full when he put his penis into it.

It happened when Liz let him go on a camping trip alone about four months earlier, in August, to get away and "rediscover his energy," she said, and she gave him a plastic storage bin full of self-help books she got at a garage sale—Wayne Dyer, Leo Buscaglia, Deepak Chopra. He took the Jayco pop-up camper to a state park in a river valley and fished for trout and hiked and burned wood and drank beer and didn't talk to anyone for five days. He didn't read any of the books or rediscover his energy, but he learned that if you leave a guy alone in a camper in an empty campground late at night and there's a twelve-pack of Heineken and a jar of mayonnaise in the mini-fridge, then that jar of mayonnaise is going to get raped.

It started earlier that day, in a campsite opposing Gary's on the adjoining loop-road, when a Hmong family had taken over the site for a picnic, and from the back end of the camper, from the pull-out bunk where Gary slept, he could see the Hmongs milling around their site. He sat inside and drank coffee and watched old gray-haired ladies, short and wide and wrinkly and wearing skirts that hung to their black shoes, stirring pots on stoves on top of picnic tables and yelling at little running shirtless kids, and the kids were watched by grown-ups who stood around the borders of the site drinking beer and ignoring the old women.

Earlier in the morning, Gary had seen the same Hmongs swimming in the river. Actually, they were sitting more than swimming. At first he just saw a bunch of heads sticking out of the water. He fished fifty yards downstream and watched them out of his peripheral vision, and then he backed toward them slowly and saw that they were in a big group in a circle in shallow water just below a rock dam. It was like they were sitting around a table playing a family game and shooting the shit, only they were in a river, their shoulders bobbing as they reached down to the bottom and pulled up crawfish. One of the young fellows held a floatable wire basket, the kind you hang off the side of a boat to throw your fish into, but these people—teenagers, adults, an old lady with a huge woven sun hat—were loading up the basket with crawfish. The kid with the basket held the opening just above the surface so the others could reach over and drop in their angry little beasts. Once, he lifted the basket from the surface, water draining off the bodies of hundreds of red, squirming buggers. All the Hmongs wore surgical gloves and Gary wanted to ask them if they wore those to protect their finger flesh from the pincers, but he didn't know how to approach them.

In the campground in the afternoon, the Hmongs were dried off and making a meal from the hundreds of crawfish and drinking beer from cans and playing lawn darts and the campground game where you tossed those rubber balls attached to strings at a standing contraption with horizontal plastic pipes, and Gary saw a fifteen-year-old girl, maybe sixteen, leaning into her boyfriend, a little skinny fellow with dirty hair who stood and reclined back against a tree. She had a nice body: thin, with perfect small tits pressing through a tight white blouse that only went down a couple inches above her belly. She wore tight black shorts and squirmed and giggled, and her skin was sweaty or wet, or whatever. Nonetheless, it had a sheen to it, and Gary imagined fucking her in the camper up on one of the bunks.

Later that night, after it was dark and he'd had a few beers at the campfire, the Hmongs had cleared out and Gary was totally alone in the campground with no visible fires or lights nearby, and since he was safe from view from others, he took off his shorts and underwear and sat in his collapsible fabric chair by the fire. It's not often a guy gets a chance to sit around naked outside. In the suburbs, it was impossible, though a week after Gary returned from his trip, during a steamy Saturday night, Liz and Gary swam at two a.m. in the kid's inflatable pool in the backyard. It was one of those Intex Easy Set above ground pools that you filled by blowing up a tubular ring around the sides and then sticking a hose in there from morning until night until the ring rose as high as it could and you were left with a puffy blue circle of water four feet deep and fifteen feet across that was fresh and clear for three weeks before turning warm and green from sun, lawn clippings and accrued fertilizer.

Gary and Liz were across the street at the neighbors most of the night leading up to the two o'clock swim, in Mark and Laura's driveway, drinking Miller Lite from cans and sitting in lawn chairs around a portable fire pit, the kind on wheels. Then they kept their buzz going at home. Liz had some wine and Gary some gin, and one moment led to the next—Danny was staying overnight at a friend's house after a *Magic: The Gathering* tournament, and so they swam around under the stars. Since the water was only four feet deep, they ran around in counter-clockwise circles to get a heavy current going, and then lay on their backs and floated around, looking up at the rotating solar system, and then before they knew it, they were standing, shivering, and sipping on gin and tonics they'd set on a metal table by the side of the pool, and they hugged gropily and wet like in old times and Liz stumbled sideways and took Gary with her into the inflated rim of the pool. Since the rim was inflated and only supported by the water underneath it, they crushed the side down and started to lean over with the tumbling water, but when they got their balance, the rim rose back up and flipped their hips and they both somersaulted onto the grass along with dozens of gallons of warm water what washed over the sides from the huge waves they'd made. They walked toward the house, peeling off their suits on the back porch, hoping none of the neighbors saw. And even though there were no kids in the house, they locked their bedroom door and banged until they were out of breath. Liz's vagina dried up from all the friction but just before Gary fell flaccid, he ejaculated a little, and since she was too tired to get up and towel herself off, and Gary started snoring, she just lay on her back with her hands behind her head, and there it was: the semen didn't drip out like usual when she sat up on her knees and spread her legs so gravity would suck it out onto a towel. Instead, it stayed in there, and that's when it happened, and now what Liz told him before she passed out in the hotel room made perfect sense. She got pregnant and didn't tell Gary about it until now because she didn't think his head was right, and it all started by Gary's cheap affair with cholesterol-free mayonnaise in lieu of the young Hmong girl.

As he sat naked at the campfire, the Hmongs long gone, he had the feeling that there might be other campers out in the dark, somewhere behind trees, maybe even some residual Hmongs, and he got paranoid that the light from the campfire would illuminate his pecker, so he stood and moved behind the chair and leaned against the back of it, his ass and balls hidden in the darkness, rubbing against the cooler air away from the fire. And the air felt good down there, and he started thinking about the Hmong girl, and what if she was over there in the dark watching him, and so he went into the camper and stood on the cool linoleum floor and stroked his dinger, and figured that since he was free and safe and hidden, he could up the ante, so he looked around for masturbation ideas and long story short, he unscrewed the jar lid and sunk his boner into a batch of cholesterol-free mayonnaise. It was gross as hell, a real let-down. If he wasn't so drunk, he could have foreseen that there would be zero friction, just goop on his dick, balls, and pubes, and so he spent fifteen minutes toweling off the grease and fell asleep in a fetal position and even cried a little bit.

This could have been a low point in his life, but he put it into perspective: in movies, there were always conflicted middle-aged guys who sneaked around and had affairs with sexy women, or even trampy women who were wrinkly and dehydrated from cigarettes and alcohol, or even guys who experimented with other guys. Sometimes these affairs lead to high drama, big fights, and other times to violence and counseling, which is all good for movies and reality TV, but Gary was not one of those guys. He was one of the middle-aged conflicted guys off the radar screen insofar as having complicated adulterous affairs. Instead, he was one of those guys whose mid-life crisis consists of creative masturbation techniques. Hollywood doesn't make movies about guys like him. That's why he had his eye on the Polish girls at the resort. He was trying to up the ante, to make a move for once in his life.

On the last night of the camping trip, Gary had run out of Heineken, so he plugged in his laptop and watched some family videos that he'd loaded onto the computer. One was of a trip they took out to South Dakota to Wall Drug and the Badlands and Mt. Rushmore in 1996, and it starts with Gary aiming the camera around from the front seat of the minivan to his four-year-old daughter Heather in the back, and she's strapped into a car seat and her blue eyes are really happy. She's sucking on a nook and spacing out into the camera. And that's when Gary decided that when he got back home, he'd tell Liz he needed to have another kid before it was too late. For some reason, though, he never got around to it. Instead, when he got back to his home, he ejaculated into his wife when she was buzzed and dozed off instead of getting up to get a towel. And so now in Florida, in controlled conditions, she gets drunk and tells him she got pregnant and then lost the baby, like it was no big deal.

The next morning, Liz and Gary and Danny drove to Weeki Wachee Springs to see the mermaids, fifty miles to the Gulf Coast on a two-lane highway through orange farms and little towns with Spanish words painted on store windows. "Equipo de música. Economico."

"We need to call Vicki," Liz said, her voice hoarse from hangover.

"I called last night," Gary said, steering with his knee. "I already took care of it."

He drank coffee, left hand quivering slightly.

"What time did you call?"

"After you went to bed, about eleven."

"Why did you call so late?"

"Because I can. Because I'm a grownup."

He said he called because he was drinking and got emotional after what Liz had told him, poor baby, and so he took a walk with his cell phone out by a fake pond behind the building that had paddleboats shaped like swans.

"You have any more questions?" Gary said. He gripped the steering wheel so hard that Liz could see his knuckle bones.

"Two," Liz said. "First, how is Vicki, and second, when are we going to see her?"

"She's not good, and we're not going to see her."

"Why not?"

"I'm going to have repeat the whole goddamn conversation, aren't I?"

Liz blinked like she had dust in her eyes. He sighed and said that his cousin Greg answered the phone and didn't let him talk to Vicki because she was sleeping because of intense doses of morphine. Greg said that Vicki had been puking all day.

"I didn't exactly get the welcome wagon," Gary said. "Greg said she'd love to see us, but we should call first to see how she was because she was having ups and downs."

"What kinds of ups and downs?"

"High and lows. Peaks and valleys. Those kinds of ups and downs."

Liz looked out the window. She shook her head.

"What're you shaking your head for?" Gary said.

"Neck pain."

"So," he said, looking ahead, "he was giving me the signals that none of the cousins were too crazy about me going up there, and to tell you the truth, I'm not too happy about it. That's my aunt up there. I have a right to see her. I mean, she's my mother's twin, right?" He looked over at Liz. "Right?"

"I don't know," she said. "If she's sick, she's sick."

"Wow," he said, rapping his fingers on the steering wheel. "What a supportive thing to say. Brilliant."

Liz refilled his coffee from a green thermos. Danny snored in the backseat. Liz shook her head again and this time didn't answer when Gary asked her why she shook her head.

"So then after he'd pretty much said for us not to drive up there, he said, 'What are you guys doing down here?' and I told him we're at Disney, and he said, 'You should go to Universal instead, keep my retirement account full.'"

"What did he mean by that?" Liz asked.

"He works for Universal. And then he said to me, 'I'm just pulling your leg, buddy'." Gary tapped the brakes when he saw a billboard with two mermaids on it. "I haven't talked to the guy in thirty years and he calls me 'Buddy,' like I'm still a little fucking kid."

Liz looked out the passenger window and grinned.

Gary said all he remembered of Greg when he was a little kid was a surfboard and that he was a cool teenager for taking a little kid out to the beach. Gary's cousins were all older than him, so he never got to know them like his older sisters did.

Liz shook her head again and Gary sipped coffee.

But Gary hadn't made the phone call the night before. He made it all up because he didn't want to drive five hours and waste a whole vacation day on a deathbed experience and everyone would be sober. Instead, after Liz was passed out and Danny was safely in front of the TV set, he went out onto the deck with a gin and thought about the Polish girls. He guessed that they worked somewhere at the resort, and since they were good-looking, probably at one of the bars or restaurants as servers. He remembered that when he and Liz and the kids ate at the main restaurant lounge, Groupers, named after the fish, when they were down a couple years ago, the wait staff was all Eastern European and they had a hard time getting their food because a bevy of Poles and Slovaks and Belarusians were getting trained-in.

He applied a few thick swaths of pit-stick to suppress his forthcoming sweat and bury the smell of chlorine. He rubbed leave-in conditioner in his hair and combed it straight back with a part in the middle, pulled on some clean jeans and a green golf shirt, even though he didn't golf, and took the elevator down three flights and then walked across the gravel parking lot to the restaurant in the common area of the resort, right next to the time-share presentation building.

The bar area was dim, and no smoke hung in the air because of the smoking ban on bars that made more than ten percent of their income on food, which this one did. Gary saw this on the local Orlando news, and even though he didn't smoke, he grumbled to himself because he didn't, as a rule, like the government intervening in people's personal affairs. One middle-aged couple sat on the opposite side of the circular bar, whispering into each other and playing video poker. No one sat at the surrounding tables. Gary took a stool and the bartender walked up to him and said, "What can I do you for?"

"Twenty bucks," Gary said, trying to be clever.

"I'm sorry. What was that?" He didn't get the joke.

"You asked what you could *do* me for, and I said twenty bucks. It's a joke." Gary's face heated up.

"My name's Michael," the bartender said, working up a smile. "Get you a beverage?" He was mid-twenties and tanned, with a thick blonde head of hair and sideburns that reached his neck, and a wood-beaded necklace that made him look like he thought he might know something about Indian tribes.

"Martini," Gary said. "And a water on the side."

As Michael bent to make the drink, Gary searched around and didn't see any wait staff. There was still an hour and a half until closing and the place was dead.

"Weeknights pretty slow, hey?" he said to Michael when he returned.

"Pretty typical," he said. "It's all families up here mostly and they usually turn in early." He squinted at Gary as he placed his glass on a coaster and floated down a small napkin next to the drink.

"What do you young folks do for fun up here when the old people are asleep?" Gary said. And then he winked. And it made him feel like an old pervert. His voice sounded croaky and his armpit stink was already crashing through the deodorant. "Nothing," Michael said. "Pretty much work a lot."

Gary sucked gin and decided what the hell. He said, "I notice you folks have a lot of Eastern Europeans working here. Mostly waitresses, right?"

"Sure," he said, backing away a little, and then he smiled. "But they're off limits to the tourists." When he saw that Gary didn't smile back, he said, "Just kidding," and walked to the other side of the bar. He grabbed a couple bottles of Guinness for the couple who were leaning into each other and whispering.

Gary had another gin, a couple more, and looked around for the Polish girls. The only other time he wanted to have sex with a woman not Liz, outside of the fantasy with the underage Hmong girl, was with one of the ladies in the cul de sac, Laura, his neighbor

Mark's wife. She spent most of her time working in her yard and taking care of her sick little son Mitchell, who had kidney disease. Laura never gave Gary any signals, but one night before bed, Liz told Gary a story that he thought about a lot. Once, Liz and a gang of cul de sac moms managed to get all the men to watch the kids one night while they went out to a nightclub, a girls-night-out thing, and listened to a Van Halen tribute band. Liz said Laura was dirty dancing with a kid in his twenties, and Nancy, another cul de sac mother, said, "I can't believe she's flirting with that guy. She's got such a good-looking husband at home."

"Crazy," Gary said to Liz, and then he brushed his teeth and went to bed, but as he tried to sleep, he thought about Laura. He moved his hand over the top of his belly, and then down to his pubes and then penis, which was so soft and weightless he thought it might float off if he removed his hand.

After Gary had four or five cocktails, the grandfather of the retarded girl by the pool walked into the bar. Gary couldn't believe it. He sat up straight and put his left hand over his eye—his left eye always got weak when he drank, a "lazy eye" he'd had since he was a kid, so lazy that he literally got cross-eyed—and looked at his watch and swore it said 12:30 a.m., and this old man was just now walking into the bar.

"Beer and a shot," the old man said to the bartender. He sat three seats to Gary's right and nodded over at him. "How you doing?" the old man said.

"I've had my run."

"Come again?"

"I saw you down at the pool today with your grandkid."

"That's not my grandkid. That's my daughter." He looked forward rather than at Gary. "She's not a kid either."

"Come again?"

"She's got this deal called sporadic ALS. She's no bigger now than when she was a kid."

"Woah," Gary said. A nerve in his sternum palpitated. "I'm sorry about all that."

"She's thirty and looks like she's ten." And then the old man took a drink and didn't talk anymore. A bubble of gas swelled in Gary's stomach, so he leaned a bit to slide it out quietly but fucked it up and set off a low rumble that lingered like a sleepy dog growling from under a bed. He had another gin, a couple more, and sometime later the bartender said, "Everything good over here?"

"You're telling *me*," Gary said, tongue like a sand bag. "But what about *him* over there?" He flipped over his hand and pointed a floppy thumb at the old man, who had his head in both hands, looking down at his drink. Gary stood and leaned against the padded edge of the bar and dug in his pockets for cash and started making a pile on the bar of crumbled receipts and gum wrappers and a beer bottle caps.

Michael wiped the bar and said, "You can put this on your room tab if you don't want to fumble around for money right now."

"Am I fumbling?" Gary said. He looked over at the old man. "I'm a fumbler."

The old man turned to Gary and tried to smile, his

eyes red and wet, probably just tired or chlorine-burned, but Gary didn't know anymore why everyone's eyes were so red all the time.

Gary paused, waiting for the old man to say something profound and meaningful, like some sort of spiritual guide, but the old man just cleared his throat and looked at his beer.

Michael leaned over the bar and said to Gary, "Hey dude, there's nothing wrong with liking beautiful girls. That just means you're alive, right?"

"Girls," Gary said. And he packed a lot of emotion into the word. He meant it. He laid down some dollars for a tip and Michael swept his cupped hand across the bar and Gary's money and pocket debris disappeared and the bar was as clean as before, like he'd never been there.

Gary stumbled back to the hotel room like one of those staggering drunks in the old Laurel and Hardy movies. He was depressed about Liz's story, not because of Laura flirting with a young guy, but because of Liz's description of the bar band: a bunch of long-haired guys in their forties playing Van Halen songs. The singer was bloated, big thighs stretching through spandex pants. His belly hung out from between the folds of a black leather vest, and when he did a leg kick during the song "Jump," he grabbed a hamstring in pain and played it off as a joke, Liz had said, laughing. That didn't make Gary laugh, though.

Back in the hotel room, all Gary could hear when he walked in was the breathing of Liz and Danny, and the hum of the mini-refrigerator, so he reached down into it for a beer bottle, then tiptoed past Danny, who was splayed on the living room couch, walked through the bedroom where Liz snored, and out onto the deck. In the dark, all he could see was the pool area, some underwater lights shining up and making wave patterns on the resort buildings that surrounded the pool like the walls of a fort. And down on the first level across from him, on a patio, a man and a woman came out of their room to smoke cigarettes. They were like Liz and Gary before kids, probably early or mid-twenties. The guy was bald, probably on purpose, and he had tattoos on his muscly arms. Gary saw them earlier at the pool. The tattoos were of dragons. The wife or girlfriend was fat in the legs and lower belly but had narrow shoulders and small tits. Her hair was burnt blonde. Gary wanted to be down there with them, smoking, talking, playing cards, but then Liz walked out on the deck.

"Sorry I got so drunk," she said. "I just can't get my energy back."

"Don't worry about it," I said. "You got a good excuse."

"What do you mean by that?"

"I'm a little drunk, too."

Gary helped her back inside, got the covers over her, finished his beer and grabbed one more. He walked back out onto the deck to see if the couple was out smoking and kissing, but they'd gone back inside, probably in their hot tub drinking and screwing. Gary figured that before they knew it, the girl would be pregnant and the guy would be groaning to his buddies about having to take birthing classes. Then he'd be at bars alone at night, thinking about those times it was just him and the woman at the resort, drinking and smoking and fucking whenever they felt like it. Like that was all that mattered.

Gary sat in the metal deck chair and looked up and listened to a moth bounce around on the underside of the deck to the room above him, trying to get to the security light. It seemed like maybe his whole life boiled down to watching a moth do its business with a light. But he was drunk and the garden of his mind was totally fucked, and so he decided that in the morning, he'd get down to the pool early and wait for the old man to bring his daughter back down. Gary figured he'd help his wife give it another try, to help the old man's daughter learn how to float, because it was important. Gary was going to reshuffle his priorities.

Gary forgot all about reshuffling his priorities, though, by the time he woke up in the morning with the fingers on his left hand quivering, and that's why he was steering into the Weeki Wachee parking lot and saying, "Jesus, when I was a kid, this place was packed." The sheet of cracked gray pavement was half full with minivans and beige rental cars. Sun washed down on a row of yellowed mermaid statues that lined the main entrance. They walked by a circular Grecian fountain, one foot deep with water green from algae and full of pennies that tourists had chucked in there. A spire rose from the center of the fountain, and on top of it, a mermaid sat on a pedestal and dribbled water from her mouth.

"This fountain looks exactly like it did in the '70s,"

Gary said, bending to look into the cracks in the stone. "This could almost make a guy happy."

Liz sighed and stared at the old woman behind the glass at the ticket booth. It was up to her to get the tickets, do the work as usual. The clerk's face was leathery and her teeth looked like candy corn. Danny stood behind Liz with his hands in his pockets, tunes pulsing from his ear buds. When Gary walked up behind him, Danny glared as if he'd been interrupted while doing something important.

"You get the tickets?" Gary said to Liz.

"What do *you* think?" she said.

They walked into the park; the grounds manicured with shrubbery trimmed into the shapes of whales, porpoises, and other ocean creatures. "Here's Memory Lane," Gary said. "My dad got a bunch of pictures of me and my sisters down here."

Memory Lane was a shrub-lined path with little turn-offs where kids could get their pictures taken on plastic statues of dolphins, manatees, giant clamshells, and then they could poke their faces through openings in walls with murals and be either Poseidon or his wife Amphitrite, both of whom were crowned and had fins and big chests.

"Get up on the dolphin," Liz said to Gary. As soon as the dad checked the kid's photo on the digital screen and the little kid climbed down, Gary climbed up. The blue dolphin waggled back and forth on its metal stand when Gary put one hand on the head and raised his other arm in the air like a rodeo rider. Liz took the picture and said,

"You want to get up there, Danny?"

"What?" he said. He reached down to the iPod clipped to his jeans.

"Get up there and get a picture with your father."

"I'm thinking not," he said.

"Why the hell not?" Gary said.

"Because that would be gay."

Gary's arms fell to his side. "Christ," he moaned. "I'm just starting to have fun and—"

"Stop," Liz said. "The show is starting."

People in bright clothes carried video cameras toward the amphitheater where the mermaids were to perform their underwater show, the main attraction of the tourist facility.

"I'm gonna go find a beer first," Gary said. "I'll meet you people inside." He dismounted from the dolphin. It wobbled behind him.

A year earlier on a winter night, Gary and Liz played poker with their neighbors Mark and Laura, and after some Captain Morgan and Cokes, Laura said, "Did we tell you guys we're going to Florida? We got a package from Make-a-Wish."

"That's great," Liz said. "You guys deserve a vacation." Their four-year-old boy Mitchell had had a kidney replacement. He was sleeping in their house across the street, and Laura had her walkie-talkie monitor on the table by her beverage in case he moaned for food.

"Where you guys going?" Liz asked.

"Disney," Mark said. "I've never been before."

"I have," said Gary, dealing cards. "I went to Florida every winter when I was a kid. My dad had construction projects down there and my aunt and cousins still live there. I used to drink orange juice out of these plastic containers shaped like oranges. You guys have to go see the mermaids."

"You're so eloquent all the sudden," Liz said, then looked at her watch and gave him a wink.

Gary stopped dealing and set the deck down. "It's this place called Weeki Wachee where these ladies swim in a natural spring and people sit in an underwater theater and watch them through glass. It's one of those things where you're like, you thought everything has been thought of already, but then there's *this*. Who would have thought of something like this?" He shook his head.

"Are you going to deal?" Liz said.

Gary stared hard at her and said in a low voice, "You're always bitching that I don't get excited about anything and then I get excited about something and now you're bitching about *that*."

"I'm teasing," she said. "I want to hear the story."

He flipped a poker chip into the middle of the table and asked Mark how many cards he wanted. As the night moved on, Gary spilled the story about when he went to Weeki Wachee when he was little. He said one of the mermaids swam toward him. She could see him through the glass.

"It's like you're looking into a huge zoo aquarium," Gary said, "except there's people in there instead of fish, and it's not fake. It's natural water, the top of a huge underground spring that pumps up so much water that it makes its own river. It's incredible." He said the mermaid looked at him. She wore a flower-patterned bikini and waved at him, and as she did, her red hair floated above her in slow motion. Then she talked into a tiny microphone on a black cord. Her mumbled words floated in through the speaker system in the auditorium.

"My Aunt Vicki and Uncle Jack were there with us and they were laughing, and Aunt Vicki reached over and squeezed my shoulder. And then the mermaid said, drawling kind of the way you hear a deaf person talk, because she was totally underwater, 'Wha' o aim?' She was saying, 'What's your name?' And then I froze and looked over at my dad for help."

"'Gary,' my dad said. 'His name is Gary, like Gary Berghof, the guy who plays Radar on *Mash*'."

"Did he really say that?" Laura said. She was laughing.

"Or maybe he just said 'Gary' and then the mermaid said, 'Ew coot, Gah-ee,' which meant, 'You're cute, Gary,' and the audience laughed. My face got so hot it was like I was sick." Gary took a drink of beer. "I bet if I thought about it enough, that was probably the best moment in my whole goddamn life."

Gary said his dad kept taking pictures of the mermaid as she turned away and swam off, his Nikon 35 millimeter snapping off slide negatives like a machine gun. One of the slides, which Liz had seen—she had all their old photos digitized onto the computer—was of Gary's little-boy face, eyes wide and mouth open, staring into the water at the receding woman.

Forty years later, the theater was still musty. The seats were lacquered wooden benches and the red carpet was the flattened, hard stuff that covered movie theater walls in the 1970s. The air smelled like mildew mixed with bleach. It smelled like a lot of water had been sitting in the same warm place for a long time. When Gary sat down, Liz turned and took a picture of his face, and then he walked down to the ten-foot-high panoramic windows, the bubbling spring behind him, and held up his beer cup like a teenager at a keg party. She took his picture.

The show started and Danny tucked his ear buds into his shirt collar and stared into the water like he was stoned. The swimming girls were gorgeous and athletic and started with a performance that explained the history of the mermaid shows at Weeki Wachee. The young mermaids swam in beautiful, graceful patterns and then extended their hands to some older mermaids with thicker thighs who'd jumped into the spring and bobbed around clumsily. The older women held on to their air hoses the whole time, never letting go, thick arms chugging to hold their positions as they smiled into the windows. These were the mermaids from the past, from the '70s and '80s, brought back to swim with the new crop of mermaids.

Liz balled her fists as she listened to the history lesson. As the old mermaids swam with the new ones, a teenage boy, who was standing in the back of the auditorium talking into a microphone, recited the history lesson over the loudspeakers. He said that women had been acting like mermaids in this water since 1946 when a guy from the Navy Seals invented an underwater breathing apparatus—a hose connected to an air compressor—and fulfilled a lifelong dream of having beautiful women in his employ swim underwater for him. Elvis Presley once dropped by to see the mermaids while filming his Florida movie called *Follow That Dream.*

Florida was all about dreams.

At the end of the history performance, the new and the old mermaids swam up to the glass, stood upright in mid-float, arms around each other's shoulders like a rock band at the end of a concert, and recited their motto into the underwater speakers:

> *We're not like other women,*
> *We don't have to clean an oven*
> *And we never will grow old,*
> *We've got the world by the tail!*

Then the older women shot toward the surface and the younger mermaids slowly rose and waved to the applauding crowd as they disappeared from view.

"Was that supposed to rhyme?" Liz said. "Who cares," said Danny. "That was titties."

The boy was suddenly alert, and Liz wanted to smack him. She wanted him to wake up, but not like this, watching a bunch of fake women swimming around, pretending like they were from another world.

"I'll bet they all clean their own ovens when they get out of the water," she said.

"Huh?" said Gary, sipping his beer and smiling.

The mermaids performed for another hour. They held each other's fake fins and did loops and other choreographed moves and swam off in pairs to breathe from tubes that lay on a rock while other mermaids performed. They took turns breathing and performing.

During one of the performances, the song "Proud to be an American" played while mermaids wearing American flag bikinis swam in patterns and saluted the mock-soldiers, played by two teenage boys in desert-camouflage shorts and button-down shirts. Then two blonde mermaids rose up from behind a rock with a giant American flag held at the corners between them and waved with their free hands. Liz saw that Gary's eyes were moist and she scooted away from him on the bench. A curtain of bubbles rose in front of the windows as the song reached its end. Gary wiped his eyes and cleared his throat as the bubbles stopped blowing and the mermaids were gone.

In the next performance, one of the mermaids guzzled a bottle of soda. After each gulp, bubbles rose up from her mouth, a trick that the announcer said went back all the way to the attraction's opening in 1947. To Liz, it looked like what it looked like, a young woman giving a blow-job. And the people in the audience who leaned forward most were the dads with sunburned legs, holding video cameras and grinning.

Danny nudged Gary with his elbow and said, "I got a half a rod," and Gary laughed so hard that his belly shook and his flowery shirt started to ride up past his navel. He threw an arm around Danny's shoulders, and

Liz squinted, her finger on the camera trigger, but she didn't take the picture. It wasn't the picture she wanted. She wanted her husband and son to connect, but not over mutual partial-erections. Her husband and son were aliens. Her life had become an *X-Files* episode.

She hoped her rage was a result of her hangover, that she was overreacting.

On the drive back to Kissimmee, she closed her eyes and prayed that her husband and son were not aliens, but she didn't feel any message coming back from above that would tell her something different, so she closed her eyes tight for the next hour, pretending to be asleep in the passenger seat.

When they got back to the resort, Liz told Gary she needed to lay by the pool and maybe take a swim. She was exhausted. For some reason, he followed her.

"We'll be down at the pool, buddy," Gary said to Danny, and punched him on the shoulder. He hadn't done that for decades, it seemed to Liz.

"Where did you find your happiness all of a sudden?" she said as they walked down the hallway in their bathing suits, flip-flops smacking the carpet.

"You sound pissed."

"I'm not pissed," she said.

Liz was pissed. She'd gotten exactly what she wanted out of the trip, the reawakening of her boys, and it made her want to get into the rental PT Cruiser and drive off.

They lay back in the reclining chairs with the white horizontal rubber tubes. Gary lay all the way back, shirt still on, and curled a thick forearm over his eyes. And just as Liz's eyes were about to close, a fat Asian man walked in front of their loungers, stopped and made eye contact with her and said, "Where *to*, James? Where *to*?" in a British accent. Then he walked to another couple and said the same thing: "Where *to*, James?" Liz thought he probably got the phrase from some TV show.

Then from her side, she saw Gary move his forearm from his head and say, "Doesn't it seem like every time we've been to a hotel pool we've seen a retarded guy?"

She knew suddenly that the marriage was done, whether they stayed living together or not, especially when she saw a lady with sun-leathered skin standing in the shallow end of the pool, talking face-to-face with her husband. The woman's naked breasts were on display over the top of her bikini, which had slipped to the surface of the water, and she didn't know it. The woman's husband said nothing about the nakedness, didn't seem to notice.

Liz looked over and saw Gary sitting up on the edge of his deck chair, hands on his thighs, alert like a dog, looking like he was ready to charge into the water.

"Why isn't the fucker telling her?" he whispered in a hiss at Liz.

"I should go out there and say something," Liz said.

To their right, a group of gangly teenage boys were trying to hide the fact that they were looking at the woman's freckly tits. They stood in a circle, heads darting toward to the woman then back to each other, hands over laughing mouths.

Liz stood, but Gary grabbed her wrist and pulled her

down close to his mouth. "You can't do that," he said. "It's like a guy telling another guy that his fly's down."

"It's way fucking different than that," Liz said, and started toward the edge of the pool, but then the woman saw herself and submerged and then rose out of the pool holding the fabric over her chest.

Liz walked back to Gary.

"Have your fun?" she said to him, sitting down and toweling off her legs. "Was that better than the mermaids?"

His eyes were wide, like he'd just sustained a concussion. "That was terrible," he said. "I can't believe that guy didn't say shit." The guy, whomever he was, didn't notice his wife's own tits, and Liz realized that Gary was having some sort of personal epiphany, a moment of potential self-awareness. He looked over at her and said, "If that was you, I would have said something."

"What?" she said.

"I would have said 'your tits are hanging out.'"

She stared at him and he was silent.

"Are you serious?" she said.

"I am totally serious," Gary said.

Liz clamped her lips together, no point in talking about anything anymore. His moment of illumination came, and then it went. It punched in, and then it punched out.

When they drove to the airport on the last day, Liz driving and Gary in the passenger seat, she said, "Did you notice how rough some of these people look down here? I thought they'd look more relaxed and refreshed from the good weather."

"Maybe they're burned out from the sun," he said. "Remember my dad's skin from working on roofs all his life?"

"They look tired," she said. "Remember that lady at the ticket booth at Weeki Wachee? She just looked tired."

"Life is life no matter what the weather is," Gary said, and a knot formed in Liz's throat like she'd half-swallowed a vitamin. She wanted to reach over and punch him in the temple, but instead, she opened all the windows at once with the control panel buttons and blasted out the interior.

Engravings

Tonight will be the first time Peter Wiegard has eaten his mother's food since realizing that religious constructs are inventions designed to delude people into thinking death is not the end of consciousness, which it is. When Peter visited his folks this past summer, he told his mother Liz, "I'm an atheist" but she said, "Don't be ridiculous," and loaded the dishwasher. She coughed when Peter said that Christ's "ascension is symbolic of the human capacity for renewal, Mom. That's why it's so uplifting, literally."

"Stop talking crazy. You're a Christian just like the rest of us," said Liz, scrubbing the kitchen counter with the green scratchy side of the sponge, "and I don't mean just our family. Everybody's a Christian, even the ones that don't know it yet."

"Does that include Buddhists and Jews?"

"Yes it does, Peter, and it also includes the gays."

Peter is not only an atheist, but also gay, and Liz has never recognized the signs of gay-atheism in her son:

the way he's always crossed his fingers during the family dinner prayer or the way he's walked with a butt-sway ever since he rose from his bouncer.

Peter suspects, however, that his dad Gary knows. After he told his dad that he'd switched majors from Computer Networking to Studio Arts, Gary said, "You'd better get your teaching certificate so you can feed your life-partner and adopted kids. By then, those faculty unions will have same-sex partner benefits, so you should be fine. Remember, though, poems don't pay the bills."

"I'm not a poet. I'm a visual artist."

"You got oil in the car?"

This is also the first time Peter will bring his mock-fiancée, Amanda, to meet his folks in order to convince them he's not gay. Amanda drives Peter's blue Geo Metro northwest from an urban-artsy warehouse district, where the two nineteen-year-old opposite sex gays live together in a studio apartment, to a third-ring upper-middle-class suburb where Peter grew up.

They drive north and west past town homes, office malls, and chopped-up farm fields, mounds of construction dirt smeared with snow crust. It's a windy, cold afternoon, and slippery roads make Peter nervous, so he sits in the passenger seat and presses his legs down because the nerves in his thighs bounce.

"Just tell your folks you're gay," Amanda says. "You're a big person now."

"You're too casual," says Peter, who, though gay, does not whistle his sibilants. "These people are Congregationalists. My mom will probably have my little brother greet us at the door in a bow tie. The kid's fourteen and all he does is play wizard games but my parents made him join Toastmasters to learn how to communicate."

Amanda lights a cigar only slightly larger than a cigarette, with a white plastic filter tip. A cigarillo. "Maybe your brother is gay, too."

Amanda, a feminist lesbian Literature major, accuses Peter of painting stereotypes. She uses the verb 'painting' because Peter doesn't paint and she likes to rile him. He engraves. He is a postmodern Albrecht Durer, but instead of dense scenes of depressed angels and apocalyptic nightmares, he blends modern images of contemporary Americans from various demographics into collages that show interconnectedness. Last year, Peter made the following engraving, as described in the critical interpretive essay his studio teacher required he write:

Two transparent football fans lean over a stadium railing and hold up beers, mouths agape in touchdown screams. Their bloated figures fill the foreground, and behind and through them is a backdrop of images from a cityscape: a neglected African-American youth walking on a sidewalk in front of a boarded-up store that says, "We cash checks," a Native American adult male in a baseball cap standing in front of a sign that says "Alano Society." Etc. The African-American boy smiles as the hand of a non-threatening adult black man from a Big Brother program reaches out for him. Message: the African-American child has an active male mentor and the Native American adult male is not a drunk but in recovery, and has cycled through the steps at least twice based on the size of his coffee cup.

Meanwhile, the suburban rednecks in the foreground are large, reflecting not only literal obesity, but also the figurative manner in which they dwarf the "smaller" people in the "background," reflecting today's media coverage, i.e. tailgaters who drive in from the suburbs get more media play than urban minority children engaged in meaningful after-school activities. Though the suburban chip-eaters are large, they are transparent, while the people with real struggles are small but sharp, seen clearly, if we look, *while we cannot see the football fans because they are hollow vessels full of domestic beer and narrow ideologies.*

Amanda once questioned how Peter could engrave transparent images, and it pissed him off so much that he still refuses to show her the engraving. "It's too heavy-handed the way you're describing it," she'd said. "It practically screams, 'This is a picture about bashing stereotypes. Get it?'"

"It's not a 'picture.'" Peter's voice had risen and cracked. "It's an engraving."

Peter often yells at Amanda in a rising pitch, but she never yells back. They argue because they are Temperamental Artist Types, which is how Peter's tax-attorney uncle, Lyle, refers to them. Lyle is a stereotype, too: the Typical Suburban White Corporate Guy Who Labored Through College with a C Average and Now Has Too Much Economic Security and Thinks He Has the World By the Nuts. He wears fanny-packs to public events that cost large entry fees and believes that Jewish people own too much and that their humor is all based on worrying about unimportant things. Lyle will be at dinner and will eat two large portions even though he knows his bad cholesterol is above the normal range.

"Listen," says Peter as Amanda reaches for the radio. "My mother has dinner procedures. You need to know protocol." He'd explained much already, and Amanda either laughed darkly or sneered, which is a trait of many Embittered Lesbians. She also has lovely white teeth even though she smokes cigarillos and has no crow's feet at the edges of her eyes even though she leers. She only sleeps four hours a night because when life ceases, awareness ends. Amanda is a gay atheist like Peter. She's also a freestyle verbal poet.

"Here's a freestyle," says Amanda. She clears her throat and sits up straight. "If there are demons in the salad, say it's the best evil you've ever had. If the lasagna screams, pray for its spirit and devour. If you rebuke the food, you'll dream of serpents. Help yourself to more."

"Don't minimize this," Peter says. "That'll just make it true."

"Make what true?"

"Congregationalists pray for miracles to convert gays into heterosexuals."

"What? They do not. Just tell them you're gay. Be free to live." Amanda puffs her mini-cigar and waggles the filter over her tongue ring, which she uses to stimulate her female partners, whom, like Amanda, have no intentions of reproducing.

"The worst part will be watching TV with my dad and uncle after dinner," Peter complains. "It's a rule. We'll watch ESPN *SportsCenter* and they'll make comments about the cars in the car commercials. 'You read that review in *Consumer Reports* about the new Sentra?' The worst are Sundays when they watch golf and praise this guy named Phil Mickelson for coming close to winning the majors but not winning. They feel sympathy for a guy who makes millions of dollars a year for walking around outside and waving at people. Why do I have to respect Phil Mickelson to prove my American Maleness?"

"Good thing it's not Sunday, then."

"Worse. It's Friday." Peter runs this hand through his hair. "We have to watch baseball, which I love, and that makes it worse. I can tell you the script: the old man is going to comment on how starting pitchers nowadays are pussies because they can't throw more than ninety pitches and it's unfair that relievers make millions pitching one or two innings every three games, but then on Sunday he'll root for Phil Mickelson to make more millions. Why is it okay for old Phil to make millions playing golf but not Mariano Rivera, who saves fifty games a year?"

"I only watch the WNBA," Amanda says, and reaches for the radio dial.

"Quit the stereotypes," Peter says. "The double-standard is that most relief pitchers are Latin-American and Phil Mickelson is an Upper-Class Hetero-Anglo with man-boobs. That's the difference."

"Just tell them you want to watch *HGTV* or *Lifetime for Women*."

"You're not funny."

"You're acting so gay right now," says Amanda. "Show them you know more about baseball than straight guys."

Peter pounds the dash and laughs. "I do, and they say, 'You can't compare golfers to baseball players. That's like comparing apples and oranges,' and that's it. Debate over. Then the old man will say, 'You're buying too much liberal bullshit at college' or Uncle Lyle will say, 'What do you like best, Peter? Pitching or catching?' and then I get mad and my voice shakes and they laugh and fart and then they laugh at their own farts and say things like 'Glad I got that workin' right.' Sometimes they call me Nancy."

"That's such a gay thing to say," Amanda says. "Just tell them you're gay. And which *do* you like best?"

"What?"

"Pitching or catching?"

The nerves in Peter's thighs quiver like Phil Mickelson's breasts when he waves to the gallery. Peter can't talk anymore, and knows that if he tries, his voice will crackle like an emphysema patient who takes off the oxygen mask and attempts to communicate.

Amanda parks the Geo Metro in the driveway of the Wiegard's two-story split-level near the end of a cul de sac behind two tan minivans and a blue Lexus. She and Peter walk the shoveled sidewalk to the "foyer," as Liz calls the front porch. The door springs open to Liz's blonde hair and the light beard of Gary, who already has his Bleary-Eyed-Drunk expression on, who puts his hand on Amanda's shoulder and leads her inside and to the basement to show her his new plasma TV while Liz nudges Peter into the kitchen, where gathered around the center-island on stools is Uncle Lyle's family.

Tax-Attorney Lyle, Gary's brother, is dressed in a plaid short-sleeve button-down shirt; his wife, Terri, an Upper-Middle-Class-Home-Maker with a BA in Social Work who tutors retards on a volunteer basis in order to appear socially-conscious, picks over a cardboard plate with celery and carrots and low-fat ranch dressing. Their Insolent-and-Apathetic-Gum-Popping-Blank-Eyed-Teenage-Daughters, Peter's cousins, Luci with an "i" and Ronni, also with an "i," sit on tall bar stools at the end of the island thumbing through newspaper ads of Old Navy and Abercrombie and Fitch, which was voted Favorite Clothing Store by the students of Apple Valley High School as reported in their yearbook. The blue Lexus in the driveway is Ronni's. She and Luci drove up together so they could listen to a Lil' Wayne CD, which has a song that says, "But I admire your poppin' bottles and dippin'/ just as much as you admire bartending and stripping." Tax Attorney Uncle Lyle doesn't understand Lil' Wayne. He understands Billy Joel, though, and his favorite song is, "You're Only Human," which he and Terri listened to on their drive over.

What Lyle sees as Amanda removes her black leather jacket and hands it to Terri for hanging: a Lesbian of the Dark Poet-Type. She has short-cropped hair pressed to the sides of her skull like a helmet with two tendrils like sideburns arriving at a terminus at her cheekbones.

Her hair is dyed severe black, like death, and her earlobes are spangled with zirconium studs. She wears tight black jeans, boots, and a sleeveless black t-shirt with no logo. Lyle sees black hairs sticking from the cracks of her underarms as though two negro kewpie doll heads were squeezed up in there, but he's not surprised. He's always known that lesbians don't shave their armpits. It's a form of protest.

As the family gathers in the kitchen, Peter's fourteen-year-old brother Danny is upstairs in his room listening to death metal on headphones and accessing pornography on his computer and considering masturbating. He logs off the Internet when he hears the commotion downstairs, but not before removing the "history" files that refer to www.gaypoles.com, which is not a site devoted to happy Polish men. He enters the kitchen wearing a white dress shirt, suspenders, and bow tie. He shakes Amanda's hand and in a monotone voice, like a robot, says, "It's nice to meet you, Amanda. I have something for you." He opens a drawer, produces a transparent container full of "Hello! My Name Is . . ." conference stickers, walks toward her. He leans in close to her ear and whispers, "This is my mom's idea. She wants me to be more sociable. I joined Toastmasters to get her off my back."

"Socialization is overemphasized in this culture," Amanda says.

"Whatever," Danny says. "Just please take the damn sticker."

"No thanks," Amanda says. "I'm against name tags." She mock-yawns and then laughs. Everyone laughs back, except Danny, who says, "I think it's all bullshit."

"Danny!" Liz says in an appropriate and firm tone of one displaying good mothering skills.

Amanda snatches the sticker from Danny's hand and slaps it upside down on her forehead in order to lighten the mood.

"She's a live wire," Tax Attorney Lyle says, and winks at his nephew Peter. "I have an old lady who talks back, too." Lyle winks again, this time at Terri, who in mid-transport of a steaming tray of lasagna flips him a mock-scowl designed for public view. The scowl sends the following message: "We often quip like this in public because we have a healthy relationship."

With mystical timing, Liz calls out, "Dinner's ready."

The tabled food glimmers in its various states of moisture-release: lasagna, tossed salad, corn cake, pasta salad, milk, coffee, and non-alcoholic red wine for everyone but Gary and Uncle Lyle, who have Heinekens. Flower arrangements surround the bowls, plates, and silverware settings as though having open space on a dining room table violated one of the Ten Commandments, a wood-burned copy of which hangs on the dining room wall behind the head of the table where Gary sits, which gives to outsiders the appearance that they are church-going folk, even though Liz is the only regular church-goer, and does it more for the clubs than the theology. On the opposite wall, behind the foot of the table, is a window with white grills, lace curtains, and surrounding the window, family photographs in collage frames of the variety found on clearance at Liz's favorite store, Kohl's.

The centerpiece of the table: potpourri in a ceramic vase sizzling over a votive candle. It's held in the air by a black wire-framed contraption that rises upward out of a circular wreath-like arrangement of interwoven white bird feathers and plastic red berries.

A gust of wind slams into the dining room wall, a jolt so hard that the ten-year-old family portrait that includes Gary, Liz, Danny, Peter, and oldest sister Heather, who is twenty-one and no longer tries hard to make it home from college on weekends because it's too stressful and she is working hard on her Social Work degree, tips slightly to the right, and only Peter, the Artist of the Family, notices. Instead of noting it aloud, however, he puts his hands under the table and presses his thighs down because his nerves are popping off again.

"Oh no," says Liz, calling attention to the wind but not to the tipped family portrait. "It sounds windy out there. It must be windy."

Gary sits at the head of the table, scooting up close so his belly touches the edge. Liz sits at the foot. Lyle and Terri and Ronni take one side of the table while Amanda, Luci and Peter take the other. Liz has excused Danny from dinner to work on a speech for his Toastmaster's club and he is now upstairs with his headphones on, listening to a scream metal band while masturbating to the pornographic website he had closed when Peter and Amanda arrived. After that, he will play *Wizards* and *Warcraft* online and then masturbate again before going to sleep.

There's no chit-chat, no easing into things. As dishes

and trays begin their clockwise float around the table, Gary says, "You can't pay the light bills with poems. Amanda, did Peter tell you I was operating a machine at my company, down on the floor, and I lost the tip of my left thumb?" He extends its absence toward her while handing her a tray of buns. "Grinder accident."

"I don't write poems," Peter says. "Amanda does."

"Sometimes I go down to the factory floor and run the machines so that the employees will know I'm just a real guy like them."

"Salt of the earth," Uncle Lyle says.

"Have we prayed yet?" asks Liz.

Peter crosses his fingers under the table.

Lyle says to Gary, "Hey, I might have to take a couple weeks off work to get your taxes done."

A tax joke. Uncle Lyle has many well-rehearsed tax-related quips at the ready.

"Peter paints," Liz says. "Thank you Lord for this food. It looks almost good enough to eat."

"I don't paint. I engrave," Peter says, and uncrosses his fingers, confused why his mother didn't uncork the formal prayer before putting the food in motion or scold Lyle for interrupting her. She's usually stringent when performing. And the family portrait tipped. The patterns are shifting. "Engrave," he says. "I do engravings." His right eyelid jumps.

"*Amanda* writes poems," Liz says to Gary. "Isn't that right, Amanda? I used to write poems in college, too, before I went to work, I guess. I don't know. What church did you say your family goes to, Amanda?"

"I don't *write* poems, actually," says Amanda, but Gary interrupts.

"Like I said," Gary says, "poems don't keep the furnace blowing heat. Being artsy and whatnot is okay and everyone should get the benefit of the doubt for that kind of thing, but you better think about teaching certificates or something or you could end up living in a warehouse eating macaroni and cheese."

"We already are," says Amanda.

"I don't want to teach." Peter's voice rises. "I want to engrave."

"Where can you sell your paintings, though?" Tax Attorney Uncle Lyle says. A tomato-sauce smeared noodle-chunk sticks to his chin like a cold sore. "You thought about setting up an eBay account?"

"That's not the point. I'm not it in for the money," Peter says, voice rising and cracking. "They're not paintings."

"Poakchawps and appewsauce," Amanda says.

"What?" says Lyle. "We're having pie?"

"*Brady Bunch* reference," Amanda says. "Poakchawps and appewsauce. Remember that episode?"

"I know that," says Gary. "I get the reference. Did you know that Robert Reagan, the guy who played the dad, was a gay?"

"Robert Reed was his name," Tax Attorney Lyle corrects. "I knew it back then. He was too much of a listener to be a real father. Real architects don't listen to their kids the way he did because architects are left-brainers and gays are right-brainers. Well, maybe not all gays. I don't want to generalize."

"We had a gay accountant on staff one time," says Gary. "He kept it to himself, though. He knew he couldn't have any, if you know what I mean, so it didn't bother anyone."

Peter snaps, "Every conversation at this table ends up being about gays, blacks, or Jews."

"That's prejudiced to say," says Gary. "We haven't talked about blacks or Jews."

"Let's talk about movies," says Terri, smiling at Amanda and pulling her brunette hair back behind her ear as she reaches for a salad refill, a public display that shows her regard for personal health. "Have you guys seen *Avatar* yet? It's really neat."

Gary leans back in his chair and waves his hands as if signaling an incomplete pass, proclaiming, "Listen, I've hired blacks before. Remember that black guy that used to do our marketing? Good guy, and blacker than hell. He said that some other black guys just couldn't make it in the real world and that's why they went into the military. They needed structure. If you didn't keep them busy, they'd be out raping British girls."

"What?" Peter says, voice elevating. "What do British girls have to do with anything?"

"That's awful," says Liz, emitting a cough, which she does when morally offended. Once, when Peter told her his favorite movie was *Fargo*, she coughed and said, "Midwesterners don't talk stupid like that." She then wiped the corners of her mouth with a napkin.

"Hey, Peter," says Lyle. "Why do all British girls have bad teeth?"

"Is that a joke?" asks Peter. "Should I say, 'I don't know,

Uncle Lyle? Why do all British girls have bad teeth?'"

"I don't know any British jokes," says Lyle. "I just want to know why they all have bad teeth."

"The reason I bring up *Avatar*," Terri says, looking across at Amanda and pointing her thumb toward her brother-in-law, "is because it's about this guy who lives in a parallel universe." Terri rolls her eyes, apologizing for her husband being such an incorrigible, playful nuisance.

Peter's thigh nerves bubble like lava. His armpits itch.

"Listen," says Gary. "Black guys beat women. It's just a part of their culture. And that's in the words of the black guy who I hired once. Don't shoot the messenger here. I'm just reporting information."

"Jesus Christ," says Peter.

"Stop!" says Liz, voice suddenly hoarse and whispery like the cobra in *Rikki Tikki Tavi*. "Don't use Christ's name as an expression of surprise!"

"How about in *disgust*?" Amanda says.

"I never brought up Jews," says Uncle Lyle, responding to Peter's long-ago comment, just now getting it. "Why are you saying I brought up Jews?"

"I didn't."

"I'm Jewish," says Gary. "That's why I'm funny and smart."

"And neurotic," Amanda says, thinking she's entering into an irony game with Peter's father.

"Wrong!" Gary makes the *Jeopardy!* buzzer noise. "Old Peter there got the neurotic gene," and then he tumbles into his story about how his father, Arnold Wiegard, the man from whom he inherited Wiegard

Truss Construction, had been named "Arnold Hamer" at birth before his mother divorced Arnold's biological dad, Fred Hamer, and remarried a guy named "Bill Wiegard," who pretty much raised Arnold. Gary, at first, thought his father Arnold was Norwegian because Arnold said so, but once, Grandpa Arnold got loaded and told Gary the story about his real biological father and said his name was actually pronounced "Ha-*meer*," silent "H." As a result, Grandpa Arnold, and thus Gary, have Ukrainian Jew in their blood. "Jews are the smartest demographic and there's research to show it," Gary says.

"Was the research written by Jews?" says Lyle. "Just kidding. When's pie?"

To test his father's story's truth, Peter had once stolen an old photo of a younger Grandpa Arnold from Gary's collection. In the black and white glossy, Arnold stands behind the bar of a café, and sure enough: Jew-nose. Peter did the math and figured he was 1/4 German, 1/8 Norwegian, 1/8 Anishinabe, 1/4 Scottish, and 1/4 Jewish; thus, he's volatile, stoic, prone to diabetes and alcoholism, and understands amortization. Peter told Amanda he wanted to do an engraving of the café-scene and title it, "Hereditary Disposition Revisionism." Amanda told him to title it, "Jew-Nose Hamer with a Silent 'H'."

"You're not a Jew, Gary," says Lyle. "You're full of shit."

"I know how to make money, though."

"I did your taxes, Gary," Lyle calls out. "You're a hell of a lot better at spending money than making it." Both men emit laughs that lead to watery eyes. Lyle has so many tax jokes at the ready that it's almost amazing, and all of which he hears at work and attempts to memorize so that he can use them later in various conversations.

"And the money I didn't spend," rages Gary between laughs, "the Indians took." Both men laugh again, this time at an Indian casino joke. Neither man likes it that Native Americans, whom they admit that the United States government wanted to assimilate into Capitalism in the first place, are now making scads of money off of chain-smoking retired white people while at the same time stealing their fish with big nets and spears, which is unfair.

The dinner conversation becomes two-directional between Gary and Lyle and the women eat and look down at their food. Peter's thigh nerves bubble, and he's had enough. He slams his palms down on his thighs and says loudly, "I'm gay and so is Amanda and this is all bullshit."

Silence.

Amanda reaches under the table and sets her hand on Peter's thigh, and after three seconds, Gary says, "I'm gay, too, fella'. How'm I gonna tell my wife?"

Laughter all around. The wind blows again. The family portrait straightens back up, but only Peter notices.

After dinner, Peter walks to the bathroom with Amanda while Liz prepares apple pie and coffee, and Gary and Tax Attorney Lyle aim for the basement to watch ESPN.

"I'm exhausted," Peter says, pulling down his jeans and sitting on the toilet while Amanda opens the window and pulls a pack of Cigarillos from her handbag.

"Don't smoke here," he says.

"Your dad's funny," Amanda says, putting the pack back in her handbag. "He's good at irony."

"He doesn't know irony, Amanda. He's a literalist."

"Bullshit. Nobody can say that kind of crap and be serious."

"Welcome to the cul de sac."

Peter tells Amanda that she's expected to go into the kitchen and sit at the island with the females and watch Liz clean and talk about their latest purchases at places like Hollister, Kohl's, and Bed Bath & Beyond. "Don't help her clean, though. You haven't earned the right. Only Terri can help. My mother would act insulted if you started wiping something."

Amanda pats Peter's head and leaves him to his lonely toilet-squat, one he has performed a million times after a million family dinners, although he knows his bowels will not move until the Geo Metro's front tires leave the driveway. Yet he also knows that this post-dinner-toilet-squat will be his last moment of peace before he has to walk to the basement where the boys watch ESPN baseball and where he will hear, because it's engraved on his brain, either his father Gary or Tax-Attorney Uncle Lyle complain about how The Latins are taking over baseball the way The Blacks took over the NFL "except at the quarterback position" and how all of The Latins are named Rodriguez or Gonzalez, and then one of them will say, "If Harm Killebrew played today, he'd have to fight for a job." And then the men will laugh at the funny commercials even if they aren't funny, especially if they're business-related, if they sell copiers or cell phone plans in a funny way. They'll talk about the PGA and one of them will say, "Did you see Mickelson had that putt worth 150 thousand? Must be nice." And they'll make expressive faces when they fart and say, "That was good" or "That one hurt." And they'll talk about Chickenshit Liberals and Tree-Huggers and when one of them disagrees on a point, the other will say, "We agree to disagree on that one," or "Everyone's got their own way of looking at things" and then change the subject to Mexican immigrants, both of them prefacing their comments with, "I'm not prejudiced, but" and "I'm not racist either, but" and later while talking about Social Security or the Lexus versus the Acura, one of them will say, "It's like comparing apples to oranges" and thus end a debate barely begun and both will breathe heavily and one will drift to sleep as the TV speaks of beer brands and pitch selections, and Peter Wiegard will do what he has never done before: he will walk upstairs and join the ladies in the kitchen, pull a fresh sponge from the drawer, and he will wipe the counters in broad, circular motions.

The World at War

On the last day of eighth grade, I walked home from school, threw my books on the kitchen counter, and pulled a note off the refrigerator. "There's a chicken dinner in the freezer," it said, "and sometimes I think this world is another planet's hell." The sentence lodged in my brain like Barry Manilow's "Copacabana" after hearing it in the speakers at the mall, and it made me want to punch myself in the forehead until bruising appeared.

I peeled the note from the refrigerator, tucked it in my back pocket, snatched a yellow pad from the junk drawer and scribbled in left-handed penmanship: "Dear Mom, hell is other people, and I know every theme song to every show featured on TV Land." I slid it under a refrigerator magnet then grabbed a Banquet TV dinner from the freezer. I peeled back the cellophane from the apple cobbler, forked holes in the chicken compartment, and slid the tray into the microwave.

Mom didn't cook anymore because she ran a KinderCare and worked long hours, and Dad never cooked because he had serious work to do. He ate out, had cocktails, and networked. Once, he networked on my sister Heather's face when she came home with her shirt untucked and a moist grin on her face. That was three years ago when she was still at home, before college. He'd been having drinks in his study while watching *The World at War* while I was in my room upstairs, playing *World of Warcraft.* The TV vibrated through the carpet, loud as hell because Dad's hearing was sub-par.

He watched one of his favorite *The World at War* episodes, the one where the Hitler Youth looked happy and content about structure and discipline in their daily lives. Then the front door slammed and Heather staggered in, not drunk, just happy. Dad threw her up against the back of the front door and asked her if she wanted the neighborhood thinking his daughter was a slut. She said no, she didn't, and hugged him to calm him down.

One of Mom's notes said, "None of us live up to God's high ideals. Dad is not a bad man. He's just a man with frailties." And I wrote back, "We're moving on up, to the east side, to a dee lux apartment in the sky."

After two minutes, I pulled my TV dinner from the microwave because I loved to eat the crunchy ice chunks of corn. I loved the way their coolness melted across my tongue while the apple cobbler with the fine crumbling crust remained scathing hot. I sat at the foot of the table and dug in. The foot of the table was my place in the universe. Dad told me so and I believed him. He was the head and I was the foot while the rest of the family sat somewhere in the middle.

Dad wasn't home yet, but I knew he still lived there

because I saw the proof behind his chair, a path in the carpet where he paced with his cellphone. His path ran from the family room down the hallway to the bathroom where he talked while peeing. I was supposed to admire that Dad spoke to important people while urinating. It was a physical example of him being his own person. His favorite line was, "I'm my own person and I don't give a shit what anybody thinks," which he also said while preening his goatee in the mirror and sculpting his thick black hair with spray, the phone wedged into his neck like a burping baby.

I wrote a note while eating: "In the theme song of *Leave it to Beaver*, they just whistle. The same applies for *My Three Sons*, except they also snap their fingers, and that's what makes the show its own show." I turned a page in my notebook and looked across at the head of the table, where Dad sat when he was home. The pictures of my sister Heather, who was off at college, and brother Peter, who didn't live here anymore, leered down at Dad's empty seat.

Dad was home yesterday evening before seven, and we ate alone because Mom was late from work. He growled into his bowl of Campbell's chicken noodle soup. He stirred his spoon around the runny broth and cleared his throat. "A foot can't work without a head," he said, staring at me and rubbing his goatee. "You know that, don't you?"

"What?" I said, spooning a salted cracker through my yellow soup.

"You're at the *foot* of the table, Danny," he said, loosening his tie, "whereas I'm at the *head* of the table." He lifted a whiskey glass in his shaky fingers and sipped, squinting at me with dull eyes. I stared back into my broth, spooning noodles to the top before a film of scum formed. Ice cubes clinked against the sides of Dad's glass.

"A foot can't work without a head," he said. "Do you follow?" His deep-set brown eyes, like polluted river water, sharpened under his thick black hair and eyebrows. His hard stare on my forehead felt like an ice cream headache. He rested his elbows on the table and clasped his fingers, chin resting on folded hands. He shut his eyes and opened them slowly, like a professor. "A foot can't work without a head," he said, voice deep and patient.

"Or another foot," I said.

"Don't get smart." He straightened up and grabbed his spoon, held it over the soup and froze, narrowing his eyes back at me. "Do you know what I do for a living? Do you understand the responsibilities I have?"

I shoveled soup onto my tongue and swallowed. "Business owner," I said, dripping broth on my chin. "You have a lot of balls in the air." I repeated what he wanted me to say. "You juggle balls."

"Soup," he said. "I come home and make soup."

"It's fine," I said.

"Of course it's fine." He snatched up his glass, walked to the kitchen and pulled a bottle of scotch from the liquor cabinet. "I can make soup. That's not my point." He added soda water to his glass to dilute the dark liquid. He stuck his finger in and swirled. "A guy with my responsibilities shouldn't have to make soup. I mean, I can make soup, but when I *have* to make soup, I get angry. Your mother called me at work." He transformed into his Mom impression, voice high and whiny, waggling his limp wrists like a begging dog, and rolling his eyes. "She said 'Have dinner ready for Danny, will you Gary? I'll be a bit late tonight, n'kay? Thanks'."

His body slumped and he leaned on the kitchen counter. "Do you have any idea what I'm talking about, Danny? Do you know that if I hadn't taken over your grandfather's business, I would have been the first college graduate in my family? Do you realize that? Do you understand what it's like to be a wolf? Do you *know*?"

I knew. Dad was a wolf, like Harry Haller in *Steppenwolf*, a book he had to read back in college for an Intro to Lit class, before he dropped out and took over the business from Grandpa Arnold. It was the only "literature" he had on his bookshelf. The other books were *What Color is your Parachute? Jonathan Livingston Seagull*, and *As a Man Thinketh*. He never talked about those. Instead, he talked about *Steppenwolf* to demonstrate his intellect.

"I'll make soup," I said. "I make my dinner all the time. Chicken, fish, apple cobbler—"

"You will *not* make soup." He clutched his glass and looked in at the ice. "And neither will I. We don't have to make soup, Danny."

"We don't have to make soup?"

"I'm not archaic," he said, pacing, running a hand through his thick hair, strands sticking to his glowing forehead as if his perspiration were Elmer's glue, the kind we used in school when we were forced to cut animal, plant, human, and building shapes from magazines and glue them to construction paper. *Collages*, the teacher called them, "the pasting together of various shapes and materials not normally associated with one another," unlike in life, where associations existed between everything.

"Your mother and sister think I'm archaic." Dad paced the kitchen.

"They think what?"

"Archaic. Old-school." Dad almost never talked when Mom or Heather were in the house; instead, he clenched his glass and slunk into his office to watch TV. When it was just him and me, though, he monologued, because I usually had on my ear buds anyway, but this time I let them hang on my shoulders. "I'm not archaic," he said. "I'm a forty-four-year-old owner of a corporation and I had a Vice-President who was a woman and I even bought her that *Men Are from Mars, Women Are from Mars* book for Christmas." Dad's ex-VP, Elaine—she resigned a couple years back—looked like Pamela Anderson from Baywatch and laughed at most of Dad's jokes. During a Christmas party at our house, I saw her hanging on him in the basement, after everyone was drunk. Dad was drunk, too, and just sort of stood there swaying and grinning. The only other Elaine I knew was the one from *Seinfeld*, the only female character on the show. She was smart, insecure, and manipulative.

Dad drained his glass.

"I have integrity," he said, which the dictionary defined as "adhering to strict moral and ethical principles." He reached in a drawer for cigarettes and slapped the pack hard on the counter. A nerve jumped between my eyes. "You make implied terms on execution of a contract and live by them. You do not change terms without full agreement of the other partner, right?"

"Okay," I said. He was pissed because Mom had gone to work full-time and accepted a promotion to be the Director at a KinderCare operation.

He lit a cigarette. "And I have not 'checked out.' God, that bothers me. I just have *work* to do."

Dad never really worked, though. He didn't need to since he owned the company. Mostly he slept, but when he was awake, his body gave off a dry heat like he had a furnace in his torso.

He snatched up his drink and walked through the living room to his study, his untucked white shirt hanging down his ass. After he slammed the door, I heard bombs drop and screaming planes explode onto the decks of aircraft carriers. Japanese Zeros. Watching *The World at War* was Dad's favorite peacetime activity. He had the whole DVD series in his cabinet, along with two Ruger .357's he inherited from Grandpa Arnold. I could hardly lift the pistols when I broke into his study and snooped, which I did every now and then, and I always cleaned the fingerprints from the handles before I lay them back on their purple velvet pads.

Dad wasn't home tonight, though, so I could relax and eat my Banquet TV dinner. I stared past his empty seat, at the living room wall plastered with family photos of aunts and uncles and cousins we never saw anymore. The high school graduation picture of Heather was right near my seventh-grade photo from last year. We grinned through our greasy acne-skin, laughing at Dad behind his back. He felt Heather's blue-eyed stare.

Heather's blue eyes came from Mom. Peter had hazel eyes. I was the only one with Dad's brown eyes. Peter also had a tall, skinny body like Mom, sandy blonde hair and high cheekbones, while Dad and Heather were wide-shouldered like athletes and had brown hair. They also had chubby fingers while Peter's and Mom's were long and artistic. Dad thought my brother Peter looked too feminine and once when we were all at the table eating, back when it was important to Mom that we pretended to have family time, back before Peter "came out," I can't remember what Peter said, but Dad said, while looking down into his food, "I think we have ourselves a little sausage jockey over here."

I can't remember what Peter said to get him to say that, but there was no question that he called my brother a "sausage jockey," so after dinner, I Googled the term and the *Urban Dictionary* defined a "sausage jockey" as "Someone who literally likes to ride the sausage of another male," which was confusing to me at first because males don't have "literal" sausages since "sausage," in this case, is a figurative term for an erect penis, but then I understood what Dad was going after when later my brother admitted that he was, as my dad once said, "as gay as a three dollar bill."

Heather was a freshman at college getting her degree in Social Work, but still came home once or twice a month. She came home from school three weekends ago when Dad was at a conference in Las Vegas. She glued her eyes to the front door and listened for car door slams, her bones tensing and quivering like tuning forks to every noise. Her nerves were hard-wired for foot-stomps. Dad liked to slam doors and show up at odd times with his tie undone and sweat on his forehead. But he didn't come home that night, so Heather took time to counsel me on the meaning of Dad's aberrant behavior. She threw me in her Toyota and drove me to Denny's. She ate salad while I had a vanilla malt and a double cheeseburger.

"Mom and Dad have a lot of problems," she said.

"But are they their own people?" I asked.

"No," she said. "I don't think so. But Mom isn't crazy. She's just got the frailties of a human being, and that can't be helped." Heather was in college to learn how to say appropriate things to emotionally troubled people, so I fished for more words.

"They fight all the time," I said, spooning malt from the metal container into a glass. My fingers stuck to the cold sides.

"It's not your fault that they fight."

"Who said it was?"

"No one," she said.

"Then why'd you say it like it could be true?"

Heather's empty chair was to my left. Mom had no chair because she was off making sure the infants and toddlers all got picked up by their legal guardians, and when she was home she was busy getting the things done that would never get done if she didn't do them. One of her favorite lines was, "I am not a slave," which she often shouted while scrubbing the kitchen floor with Clorox. She always used Clorox.

Once, she caught me reading *Playboy* magazine in the garage and I said, "This isn't a *Playboy*," even though it was and I'd lifted it from Dad's office, and she said she believed me because she had to protect her sanity. Mom had clean blonde hair like the women in the magazine. She was slender and smooth-skinned and talked in a breathy voice. She hugged me and told me it was okay for young men to respond to their tingling groins, and that I shouldn't be ashamed.

"Why would I be ashamed?" I asked. "I was reading an interview with Johnny Depp." I really was. I was also in another planet's hell.

After dinner, I went to my room and shut the door. Mom and Dad usually got home around six and "made love" by nine o'clock. "Making love" was a term I knew from a college textbook Heather made me read called *Living a Healthy Sex Life: A Guide*, and I masturbated to black and white sketches of nipple-nibbling heterosexual couples. A passage said, "Partners often enjoy painful acts of intercourse while others receive pleasure by fantasizing about pain during acts of penetration or by talking dirty." But when Mom and Dad did it, it always sounded like planes slamming into aircraft carrier decks.

I threw the empty Banquet tray in the garbage and

walked up to my room. I lay in bed and wrote a letter to Heather, in red pen. "We got different strokes to move the world, even if this world is another planet's hell!" The legal pad sounded like thunder as my ballpoint pen ripped across it. "Just the good ol' boys, never doin' no harm!"

Sometimes when I couldn't articulate my thoughts, I conjured up *Diff'rent Strokes* and *The Dukes of Hazzard* or other classic TV Land shows to help clarify my feelings. Mom said that "making associations between things" was helpful to understanding the world. She'd put a clipping under my door the night before that read, "Freedom hath a thousand charms to show/ That slaves contented never know." It was her first rhymed quotation, but the content of the words seemed grave, which meant, "Having weight or importance; requiring serious thought." I always thought gravely, so I wrote back: "I can name the real names of every character on every show currently in syndication on TV Land or Nick at Nite."

The front door slammed. It vibrated my mattress springs. I plugged my noise-cancelling headphones into the TV, clamped them over my ears and lay back. I turned up the volume with the remote to kill the living room "lovemaking," but kept it low enough so I wouldn't miss anything grave.

"I've had it," Dad yelled. "I'm done." I could hear the booze in his voice.

I'm getting tired of hearing this," Mom yelled.

"I mean it, goddamn it."

"Then do it instead of talking."

"You'd like that."

"Don't do me any favors."

"The only reason I'm staying is for Danny's sake."

I turned up the TV. Johnny Fever was passed out on Mr. Carlson's couch because he'd had a rough night of drinking. *WKRP in Cincinnati* reflected timeless themes. Johnny Fever needed treatment. If Johnny Fever were real and living today, he'd be on *Celebrity Rehab* like Bobby from *Taxi*. The bad volume rose down the hall but I didn't have controls for that. A pause, silence, then hot breaths, the gusty snorts of angry animals. The liquor cabinet hinges squeaked. I turned off the TV and didn't know why. I never crept out of the closet until they made moaning bedroom love and went dead. Usually I stayed in the closet all night.

The noises arrived: thumps in the floor and on the hallway walls; sharp, muffled voices from Mom and Dad's bedroom; a strange, automatic mumble from my own throat. It popped up sometimes for no reason, like a bubble. I pushed open the door, stood and stretched.

Mom once wrote to me, "The wicked often work harder to go to hell than the righteous do to enter heaven," and I wrote back, "It's you girl and you should know it. We're gonna make it after all." But Mom never commented back on that note. She did her own thing, like Mary Richards from the *Mary Tyler Moore Show*. I saw a documentary about Mary Tyler Moore that said, "She was not a widow, had no children, and was working because she wanted to build her own life and career. She

spawned another career woman, Rhoda Morgenstern."
Mom also spawned a career woman, my sister Heather.
The Mary Tyler Moore Show evolved into *Murphy Brown*
and then into *Suddenly Susan*, starring Brooke Shields.
And then nothing significant happened after that.

Mom would have regretted having told me to make
associations if I said that her relationship to Heather was
similar to Mary and Rhoda's. It might be hurtful because
Mary Richards was *neurotic*, which meant, "having a
psychoneurosis," and the definition of *psychoneurosis*
was "an emotional disorder in which feelings of anxiety,
obsessional thoughts, compulsive acts, and physical
complaints without the evidence of disease, in various
patterns, dominate the personality."

I knew Mom had a *neurotic psychoneurosis* because
just before Heather had taken me up to the Denny's that
night, I heard her and Mom talking at the kitchen table.
Coffee cups tinkled and chairs shifted. I listened from
the hall as Mom leaned over the table and whispered
to Heather, "Last week, I was so preoccupied with your
father's problems that I binged and purged. *Twice.*"

She accented the "twice" part. I didn't see it but I
imagined Heather shutting her eyes in sympathy and
reaching over the table to hold Mom's cold hands. Mom's
hands were always cold.

I opened my desk drawer, scooped a pile of Mom's
notes into a shoe box and read them aloud because the
TV volume wouldn't climb high enough to drown out
the noise, even when Venus Flytrap was yelling at Les

Nessman for sitting on his pimp hat with the feather in it. I lay in bed and rummaged through the crumpled yellow notes of Mom's brain. I read, "Those who deny freedom to others deserve it not for themselves," and a voice from the living room said, "Then do it, goddamn it!"

"A good marriage would be between a blind wife and a deaf husband," I read, and then walked down the hallway, past the noisy lovers' bedroom, down the stairs into the family room. I picked up the phone and dialed.

"Is Heather there?"

"She's sleeping," said Keith, her fiancé, whom I'd never met in person but who talked to me like he knew me. "Is this Danny? Hey, wait a second and I'll wake her up." Keith was a counselor-in-training, like Heather. "Hold on, Danny. Stay on the line."

More crashing upstairs, moving toward the staircase. The voice on the phone crackled. "Danny?"

"Heather," I said. "I just read something. Listen. No man thoroughly understands the truth until he has contended against it."

"What are you talking about, Danny?"

"Who is more foolish, the child afraid of the dark, or the man afraid of the light?"

"Where's Mom? Put Mom on, Danny."

"Faults are thick where love is thin."

"Are they fighting?"

"A tendency to self destruction seems inherent in the overdeveloped human brain."

"Who said that, Danny? Speak."

"If one has truly lost hope, one would not be on hand to say so."

"Shhh, Danny, listen to me."

"Mom wrote this one to me twice," I said. "In the fight for survival, a tie or a split decision simply will not do."

Storage
(2003)

Last week, we played out the deathbed scene. It wasn't a life-changing experience, but with my dad dead, my tool collection officially tripled. I have enough power drills to arm a framing crew, which I do in fact arm, since I run a framing crew. I run many framing crews. We're the guys who put up the outlines of houses—braces, trusses, etc.—and then other crews come in for the interior and surface work.

Today's my last day off work. I took the week off for arrangements—ordering the box, funeral logistics, church reception, nodding at lawyers. Today's my last day to get shit done around the house before going back to work, so I open the kitchen cabinet next to the dishwasher and extract all the food storage containers and pile them on the counter. I open another drawer and pull out all of the lids and pile them next to containers of various sizes from small transparent cubes to large oblong orange ones with vacuum-sealable lids for foods like brownies and nachos. Some of the containers seal in moisture while others preserve crispness.

"Where are all the goddamn lids?" my wife Liz always yells. "I can't find a lid to match a container." That's why I'm taking care of this problem.

I match lids to containers, and of thirty-seven lids and forty-three containers, I find only twelve matches of containers to lids, which makes my armpits suddenly burn like a gas grill and itch like mad. Just before I'm about to crash my fist into the refrigerator, my five-year-old son Danny screams and I hear falling objects pound his closet floor upstairs.

"Hey, Dad," says my ten-year-old boy Peter, walking into the kitchen. "I'm going over to Kimmy's to play Xbox."

"Who's Kimmy?" I say.

"Jimmy," he says.

"I swear to God you said Kimmy."

My oldest kid Heather is in the backyard with a friend, jumping on our trampoline. I need to get back there and WD-40 the shit out of the springs. They're old and dry and squeaking like hell.

Last Friday when I got to the hospital after work, I knew my dad was dying because he had scared little child-eyes, except they weren't white and clear like kids' eyes. They were yellowed, almost brown, because his kidney and liver were shutting down and shit was filling his blood, and I said, "You want the baseball game on? Santana's pitching tonight."

Dad mumbled through the mask that cupped his mouth and nose and pushed in and pulled out air. I couldn't find the right TV station. Even the ICU, where terminal people went to die, had the deluxe cable package. The biggest lesson I learned from my dad's deathbed scene: people about to die still care about what's on TV.

"Norty tree," Dad said, voice limp like a wrist through the incoming and outgoing air. At his house on the lake, he got the games on channel 43. The nurse came in and said, "Lift the back of his head. I'll take this thing off so you two can talk. You're the son?"

"Norty tree," Dad said again, this time closing his eyes because of the effort.

I reached behind his head and lifted. The back of his neck felt like fish skin hardened by sun. Dad was a roofing contractor all his life, even after he opened his own truss construction plant. He had half the sun's energy stored in the back of his neck. His skin still released heat. The nurse pulled off the mask. I let his head fall back. He panted for air.

"Santana's pitching tonight," I said.

"Get ice cream for the kids," he said. "I got chocolate and vanilla. Where's the kids?"

"They have chores tonight," I said, lying. Bringing the kids to a deathbed scene was too much work. I'd have to pay attention to Dad and watch the kids at the same time, make sure they didn't start screwing with sensitive medical equipment. Also, my wife promised to watch some neighborhood kids because the parents were going to a church function and I'd worked sixty hours through

Friday and was lucky to get off by five so I could see Dad, who'd been in the hospital since Wednesday, so long story short, I was tired and couldn't deal with the kids.

I sat on a little metal chair in the corner, off the foot of Dad's bed. He was way up high and I could just barely see his head angling down at me, his cheek flesh scrunched up as he tried to make out my shape, and I laughed at a quick thought about the Hallmark Hall of Fame movie endings where a sensitive son would hold his dad's hand and whisper, "What's it like, Dad?" And then pause. "Dying, I mean? What it's like?" And the dad would look his son in the eyes and say, "It just feels right, son. No more pain."

But instead I said, as I fiddled with the remote for the TV, "You can't get sick on me now. I have to finish that tile work behind your stove."

"I got the glue and grout over there," Dad said. He pointed his limp yellow fingers at a wall of white cabinets full of medical supplies. He thought he was home.

I didn't hold his hand the way my sisters did when they came into the room later, one standing on each side of the bed and squeezing his leathery mitts over the bedrails. If I held his hand, he'd know he was dead.

I figured out the remote control and got the game, the Twins against Tampa Bay. I wanted a more historic rival like the White Sox or the Tigers for Dad's last game, but we got the fucking Devil Rays. Life is bullshit, and so is death. That's also a thing I learned.

Now that things have slowed—we're done with the

paperwork—I can get to projects. Before I organized the food storage containers, I'd been on the toilet reading an article in *Better Homes and Gardens* on how to build a backyard Japanese garden. I always read *BHG*, which Liz subscribes to, when I'm taking a dump. Though my next project was to wrap our two-tiered deck around the side of the house and install a recessed hot tub, I'm vacillating on putting a meditation garden there instead.

Danny is still screaming and sitting on the floor holding his head when I walk into his closet, which is stuffed with toys. At the far end are four shelves packed with bins of Hot Wheels tracks and Legos, and the top shelf is usually packed with board games, but not now. They lay on the floor around Danny, parts loose. I want to rearrange his closet, but first I need to determine the number and sizes of storage bins needed in order to house his loose toys, the ones without boxes beyond the board games, which since most are rectangular, fit nicely on the top shelf, until now, when he climbs up and pulls the stack down, including a Battleship game, on his head. He's holding his head. The blood on his fingers looks like watercolor paint.

Many storage bins now have latches. For some reason, though, Danny has trouble with spatial reasoning and fine motor skills. He can't work latches. Once he got stuck on the deck in the back and pounded the glass. Instead of opening the sliding glass door for him, I yelled, "Press the button down, Danny, and push to the left."

"It's too hard."

"It is not," I said. "Just try it. I'm not going to open it for you. It's inappropriate for you to keep pounding on the glass. One day you're either going to crack the glass or put your hand through it, and I don't have time to take you to the hospital."

"It's too hard."

Dad didn't open up or get reflective on me as he died. Instead, he kept saying, "Get the chisel and the scissors." I looked at the nurse, but she shrugged and drew some blood from his fingertips. Then she asked him if he wanted more morphine.

He nodded yes and then no. "In the drawer over there," Dad said. "The chisel and the scissors."

"What chisel and scissors?" I said loudly, like a dumb guy addressing a retarded kid.

"In the drawer," he said, breathing hard. He shut his eyes and winced.

The nurse grabbed my elbow and pulled me outside the room. At the main desk, she showed me numbers on a piece of yellow paper on a clipboard. I nodded when she said, "Understand?" His blood was filling with poison. Maybe he figured he could fix his guts himself if he had the chisel and the scissors. He always fixed his own shit.

When I walked back in the room, some cousins stood by the bed. They wore sweaters like they'd just come from church. Dad's eyes were closed and his hands were bouncing at the wrists, drawing circles in the air.

"Is he seizing?" I asked the nurse.

"He's fishing," said my cousin Tom. "He's cranking

a fish reel." Tom was thirty-three, only a couple years younger than me, and he said something like that. Jesus. I shook my head. Whatever makes a guy feel better, I guess.

I shook Tom's hand. "Good to see you again, Tom."

"Me too. I just wish the circumstances were different."

Tom and his wife and two kids stood between me and Dad. "Is he going to wake up?" one of the kids said. Another said, "He's got good color" even though his skin was piss-yellow. Those kids were ten-years-old and they walked around the room straightening things up and making comments like they'd done this before, like professional deathbed participants.

I wash Danny's cut and then apply a cold Ziploc bag full of ice cubes to the back of his head as he whimpers into the bathroom mirror. "Read a book and hold this on your head," I say, and then go work on the yard. I push the mower at northwest-to-southeast angles, mulch bag attached. Next, I put on my leather gloves and pace the lawn for outlaw leaves, bending and squinting down, parting the stubbly grass blades with a forefinger. When I spot a diced leaf-fragment, I snag it like an eagle spearing a trout and deposit it in a garbage bag in my left hand. Next, I move toward the three pine trees that flank the side of the house on the corner. My three pine trees are rooted in circular rock gardens, which I cleanse of leaf fragments, and then I strain leaves from the gutter. I sit on the curb, ass on shaved lawn and boots in the street, reaching down between my legs to haul up sopping leaf clumps before they clog the street drain. A guy can never be too careful. The last time I let the gutters go, I had to have the basement floor drain snaked. The utility room flooded like a trailer park.

Dad had two of everything in his garage—lawn mowers, weed eaters, power washers, paint guns, air compressors. He had smaller junk, too, like tools and boat parts, life cushions, depth-finders, fishing poles, and he'd also spread stuff like bolts, wire spools, and trailer hitches out on workbenches and rusted metal shelves that he spray-painted gray. He liked to see his stuff without having to dig through shit, everything in plain view: nuts and bolts, trailer hitch balls, electrical outlets, plumbing pipes.

"You need storage bins," I told him a week before he died. We were in the garage getting bungee cords to tie down the wood-chipper in the trailer I'd brought over to help him clear some brush and chip garden mulch.

"I hate digging through bins," he said. "I don't have time for that shit."

"A lot of storage bins are transparent," I said while scanning a tool wall covered with metal saws, screwdrivers, pliers, rolls of electrical, masking and duct tape.

"I know it," he said, "but it's not like they're clear. You can only see shapes and shit, and I'd rather see what I need without all that shit in the way."

"You can label the bins," I said.

"I don't have time for that shit."

"Well then fuck it, Dad," I said, walking out

of the garage with my hands up, pissed off at him that he wouldn't let me help him. That was the last time I saw him before he was in the hospital.

I've been remodeling our split-level rambler where we sit up on a rise looking straight out over into a cul de sac that's called by all the folks who live there, "The Sac." We find that funny because of the connection to a ballsack, like testicles. We live in a nut-pouch. Most of my containers are polyethylene. Right now I'm converting our basement into a playroom. I'm building a storage shelf system from pine planks in order to accommodate the largest bins, one of which will house Danny's Hot Wheels race track and another a Hot Wheels train set and a bin of Thomas the Tank Engine toys: cases of die-cast trains and track; wooden trains and track; a depot. He doesn't play with these anymore, so when we have time, Liz says she'll set up an eBay account.

At the funeral home, the wife and I arranged for the service, and from the laminated three-ring binder that the funeral director handed me, I chose a pine casket stained almost red. This casket would then fit into a large rectangular cement container. The pine still smelled wet and fresh like it was just cut. I don't like thinking about the tomb, but that's what it is. Call it what it is. Instead of the body going into the earth, it liquefies. I don't know what happens after that and I'm not interested in knowing.

Since we moved in here six years ago, just before

Danny was born, I replaced the door locks, installed a new garage door opener, dishwasher, dishwasher disposal and under-sink water filter, painted the kitchen, living room, dining room, both bathrooms; wallpapered both kids' rooms and decorated both by wild jungle themes, complete with a rainforest mural of monkeys and curly green snakes that fills three full walls airbrushed by my wife's friend who has a B.F.A. in Art and now works as a receptionist at Land O'Lakes; replaced the kitchen countertops with marble, replaced the linoleum kitchen floor with hardwood, laid down new carpet in the dining room and living room and upstairs hallway that connects the bedrooms; painted the house exterior a darker beige; finished dry-walling the garage interior, dug up a twelve-by-ten section of the lawn for a garden, which I later tilled, dug down further, walled with landscaping logs and poured in fifty bags of white sand for a kid's sandbox; next, I built a fire pit in the yard, and I'm just now finishing the basement playroom with wall-to-wall storage shelves. All this while working full-time and trying to be there for my kids. And wife.

After I get done with the lawn, I power-wash the deck and manage to clean the top portion. Then I tidy up and take Danny to Dairy Queen to make his small head wound hurt less. On the way we stop at Menards for a particular hose adapter so I can fix the leak in my power washer, and on the way home, pick up a pre-cooked rotisserie chicken from Rainbow Foods and eat the bird on the deck and look at the clouds for a minute.

Danny goes off to his room to play video games. His head seems to be okay after the Dairy Queen. My wife is at her sister's, scrapbooking. The boxes with the detachable lids are the best even though more elaborate models now exist with attached lids, the advantage of which is that they do not get detached and lost. However, I like the option of completely removing the lid should I choose to. It's good to have a choice.

Five hours before he died, Dad said, "I need my teeth." His lips curled over his gums, flapping in and out with the pressure from the breathing machine. He'd called an ambulance the day before after stomach pain made him fall off his deck and break four ribs on a retaining wall that I just put in last summer. "I need them for the morning," he said, "or I can't eat the toast."

Since Dad was Catholic, we had the nurse call in a priest. The one on call was a short fat guy with a high-pitched voice like Doogie Howser M.D. He stood on the other side of the bed and said to Dad, "Hello, Sir, I am Father Steve."

Father Steve yelled like Dad had a hearing problem.

At 11:21 p.m., the doctor called the front desk and asked for me. He asked if I wanted any "extra measures." I told him no, to pull the tubes, so they did, and they gave Dad more morphine and turned down the lights and we listened to him breathe. Then I kissed his cold forehead and heard a sound deep in his lungs, a long sandpapery breath like the white noise from a radio between stations. It came from somewhere deeper than the lungs. I held hands with my sisters and the priest, each of whom held hands with Dad. When we hit the Lord's Prayer, I moved my lips. The last thing Dad said was, "I'm nervous," and the nurse said, "I can take care of that," shaking a vial of morphine like a dealer.

I sit on the deck and drink coffee. I can't total it all. The clouds look like clouds. If Dad were looking down on me—which he's not—he wouldn't like to see me crying. It's a safety issue. Wear your protective goggles, never drink before work, go easy on the coffee, get plenty of sleep, and keep your personal life out of the house you're working on. Since I've got a couple hours alone, I'm going to put the new attachment on the pressure washer and finish cleaning the deck before the sun goes down.

Acknowledgments

Thank you to the Loft Literary Center in Minneapolis, and especially The Loft's Mentor Series and Jerod Santek. Thank you to my Creative Writing teachers at Minnesota State University Mankato, and to those who have generously critiqued many of these stories: Swati Avasthi, Heather Bouwman, Michelle Freeman, Heather Goodman, Pete Hautman, Jim Redmond, Mattox Roesch, Corey Quick, Emily Van Der Veer, and especially Eric Braun.

Thank you to my supportive collegiate colleagues, with whom I am honored to work, and to my early mentors who told me how to proceed: Philip Bly, Chet Corey, and Bill Holm. And a special thank you to Philip Dacey, who not only encouraged me, but taught me the practice.

Thank you to my mother for getting me get a library card, and to my wife and children for their love and support and good humor.

My greatest gratitude goes to Paula Bomer for her belief and insight into these stories, for making this book possible.

www.scottwrobel.com